KU-254-255

June Oldham

Enter Tom

PUFFIN BOOKS

For Clive, in recompense for all
the neglect lavished upon him

Puffin Books, Penguin Books Ltd, Harmondsworth, Middlesex, England
Viking Penguin Inc., 40 West 23rd Street, New York, New York 10010, U.S.A.
Penguin Books Australia Ltd, Ringwood, Victoria, Australia
Penguin Books Canada Limited, 2801 John Street, Markham, Ontario, Canada L3R 1B4
Penguin Books (N.Z.) Ltd, 182–190 Wairau Road, Auckland 10, New Zealand

First published in Viking Kestrel 1985
Published in Puffin Books 1986

Copyright © June Oldham, 1985
All rights reserved

Reproduced, printed and bound in Great Britain by
Hazell Watson & Viney Limited,
Member of the BPCC Group,
Aylesbury, Bucks

Except in the United States of America, this book is sold subject
to the condition that it shall not, by way of trade or otherwise, be lent,
re-sold, hired out, or otherwise circulated without the
publisher's prior consent in any form of binding or cover other than
that in which it is published and without a similar condition
including this condition being imposed on the subsequent purchaser

Chapter One

He saw her on the second afternoon of the autumn term. At ten minutes past four to be precise, he recorded later.

What halted him, literally brought him to a standstill in the middle of the corridor, was her hair. Polished ebony, it fell straight from the parting and shawled her to the waist. He watched the thick mass lift and settle to the rhythm of her steps as she came towards him, then, under the fringe, he saw the colour of unflecked irises, a disconcerting blue.

Quickly he worked out an insertion for his diary, not yet purchased: 'A sensational end to a day in which Olly Hardy had spent all of forty minutes analysing a four-line stanza, Nanny Childe had been unimpressed by my essay on Bismarck, Kate had failed to be amused by a witty reference to her peeling sunburn, and an attempt at promoting Anglo-French relations had not been appreciated by the French *assistante*.'

She passed him and he turned to follow her, careful to maintain a discreet gap. Generally there was no difficulty in chatting up members of staff and new ones relieved the boredom, at least for a few weeks. But he did not feel quite capable of catching up with this one and entertaining her with erudite and amusing conversation, partly because the muscles in his legs had degenerated to slack elastic (he must be out of condition) and partly because he could think of nothing to say. The mind was a complete blank; he was at a loss for words. Such clichés were usually a healthy irritant and stimulated the adrenalin, but today they failed.

Her hair glinted as she walked. Between it and the high boots was a skirt, full gathered, made of fine translucent cloth, and the pattern of lilacs, pale greens and soft yellows swayed in the draughts. 'Fluttering and dancing in the breeze,' Tom murmured. Third Form stuff and suddenly applicable, but hardly an appropriate form of introduction.

She must be going home soon. Suppose he hung about, offered to carry her bags. But that was ridiculous. Something more subtle was needed. He could wait until she left, then drive up, roll down the window, thrust out his head, 'Can I give you a lift? No, no trouble at all. You're new, aren't you? How are you finding things? Of course, this is not exactly a throbbing metropolis, but it has its compensations.' Perhaps she would ask him to supply them.

The only trouble was, he had no car. But Reg Grimshaw had come this morning in his dad's. He would let Tom borrow it. R.G., Sixth Form veteran, had a democratic attitude to possessions: you lent him your brains occasionally and he lent you his hardware.

In the car, things would be easier, more informal. Chat flows effortlessly while, with unfaltering precision, your hands flick switches or glide smoothly through the gears. He would have to ask R.G. for a quick briefing, particularly on hill starts.

They had reached the staff room and Tom became aware that she was carrying a pile of books. Without instruction, the muscles in his legs tightened. He sprang forward and latched his fingers over her load. Simultaneously the door opened and another pair of hands descended upon the books. A slight tussle developed, during which the woman made admonitory noises and the man, by shoulder and elbow movements – perfected, Tom decided, in bars, clubs and enviable joints of unimpeachable sleaziness – contrived to insinuate his bulk.

'Watch it,' Cliff Turnbull growled.

Tom did so. In fact, it was hard to miss: twelve stones of prime condition flesh, the visible parts of which were covered in tough hairs. It did not appear an auspicious moment to claim a prior acquaintance with the woman. Tom released his grasp.

In the lavatory he indulged in a less dangerous punch-up – kicked the pipes, pummelled the towel dispenser, flushed the cisterns and rattled the taps – while pounding out unprintable abuse of scabrous, scatological, sycophantic, simian Science masters who were over-hairy, over-muscled and over-sexed.

'I thought you English lot were supposed to keep your language clean,' Pin commented as he joined him.

'Not clean. Grammatical.'

'I wouldn't know the difference. What's bugging you?'

'Cliff Turnbull.'

'That could be nasty. Can't say I see much of him nowadays.'

'You're in his lab!'

'True, but I'm making a computer.'

'Have you happened to notice, Pin, in one of those rare moments when you have disentangled your eyes from the wires . . .'

'I'm not using wires, it's all . . .'

'. . . whether you've a new member of staff over there?'

Pin frowned, considering.

'A woman,' Tom prompted, 'with black hair.' He paused. Something had gone wrong with his breathing. The air coming out of his mouth was not synchronized with the movements in his chest and the sound was deafening, amplified by the surrounding tiles. He turned on a tap to add a camouflaging noise. 'And she wears high boots.'

Pin gestured acknowledgement with his free hand. 'Now you mention it, I did hear of a Miss Faulkner. Physics, I think. May have seen her around, but can't say about the boots. Sounds kinky. I'll save that up. This week I'm into pollution,' and, grinning, he expelled an explanatory fart.

Left alone, pretending to wash his hands, Tom reflected. If she did teach Physics, that was not necessarily a disadvantage; she did not look like a woman who talked shop out of school. All the same, it might be a good idea to bone it up, go to the Further Education Centre and take a crash course. What was more important at the moment was that he had not managed to introduce himself and had let her be whisked away by Tarzan Turnbull. You had to be afflicted with galloping optimism to claim that was a promising start.

Systematic planning was necessary. Tomorrow he would join her casually as she went into school. After a night's sleep and fortified with toast carefully burnt by his horrendous mother, the words would come eloquently: 'You don't know me. I'm in Sixth Form Arts.' He repeated the sentences several times, testing how far he could make them mysterious /original /sexy, but somehow they were not very gripping. They lacked punch. A musical accompaniment might help. 'You don't know me,' he yelled at the mirror.

> 'You don't know me,
> But that don't matter,'

strumming a guitar close to his chest.

> 'Come 'n get acquainted, baby,
> Step along with me.
> Brush the mornin' sunshine
> Into your black hair, baby,
> And come 'long and tin . . .
> Out-t-t-t, let's take a spin . . .
> Out-t-t-t,'

he stopped for breath and another voice finished,

> 'Just let it all hang . . .
> Out-t-t-t, while you sin . . .
> Out-t-t-t, on the cold, damp, boggy,
> Boggy, oggy, soggy . . . sheep-infested moors with
> me.

'Somehow, I don't think it will make the Top Twenty, you burk, but it could just get a mention on Pennine Radio. We ought to run some up. Earn a few quid.'

Tom smiled. One of the compensations of school, not mentionable on university applications, was Dave. 'They'd come in, too. I'm broke. How're you doing? Didn't see much of you, Dave, during the holiday.'

'Well, no . . . I was sort of tied up. I finished that novel I told you about and sent it off. I'm waiting to hear about that. Then I filled in with a few stories. Which reminds me. That girl I mentioned on the postcard from the Lakes. Nothing happened, in the end. When it came to the point, neither of us had the wherewithal, as you might say.'

'At least you got as far as having a choice!'

'Hobson's, really. To tell you the truth, she was a bit of a bore.'

'How did she take it?'

'Hard to say. She seemed rather preoccupied at the time.'

Gloomily, Dave contemplated the posters discouraging carnal excesses. 'You know,' he said, 'it's strange how it's so much easier in novels. The set-up is just right: she's going for him and he fancies her – there's never any sorting out if she's on the Pill or he's got a packet of Durex. They get on with it whether they are crossing a field knee-deep in mud or whether all they've got is one of those three-wheeled bubble cars that measure about three feet by two.'

'What novels have you been reading lately?' Tom asked.

Dave looked at him, surprised. 'My own, of course.'

That evening, since he was not in the habit of writing novels, Tom had no scene with Miss Faulkner handy for reference, so he made do with the basic details to date – a fall of jet-black hair and a train of gossamer cloth – and was moving on to the parts these covered when another woman intervened. His mother.

'I was wondering whether you would care to go babysitting, Tom,' she began.

'What, me? Babysitting?'

'That's right. I see nothing odd about that. Are you suggesting that it is a job for girls only?' She leant forward, eyes sparkling. Tom flinched. At that moment he felt unprepared to take on the town's leading apostle of Women's Liberation. 'I wonder what the Equal Opportunities Commission would say,' she added.

Rallying, he argued, 'But I'm not complaining about inequality of opportunity.'

She ignored his point. 'It would do you good to know a little about bringing up children.'

'I'm not looking round for spiritual benefits, Belinda. And anyway, I know quite a lot about bringing up children. I've been one. Remember?' As it happened, he had no objection to the job. Many of his friends did it. From what they reported it made few demands and, in addition to the wage, it had numerous attractive perks: records lent on request, porn mags in the paper rack, cans of beer, skirmishes under the mistletoe at Christmas. What he objected to was his mother's organizing this for him and the predictable arguments in her attempt to persuade him. 'I think your suggestion needs very careful consideration,' he went on thoughtfully, gnawing his lamb chop. 'Example. Is it safe for them to be left in my care? What about the effect upon me of premature exposure to them? And what about the question of my homework? Surely you are not encouraging your boy to neglect his studies?'

'You can still do your work there. The child will be asleep.'

Tom let her realize her mistake before pressing it home. 'In that case, if the child is asleep, I shan't learn anything about children.'

Victory assured, he decided. It had been customary from the cradle never to dismiss anything without a fight, and even when he intended to capitulate the trick was to do so for a reason she had not offered. So he concluded, 'On the other hand, I'd be prepared to forgo the chance to learn about child-rearing if there were financial compensations.'

Belinda looked at him wearily. 'Of course she will pay you,' she said.

The significance of that 'she will pay you' did not occur to him until he reached the house. The door was half open and, his knock greeted by a call from above, he entered and stood in the narrow hall. He looked round. Linoleum on floor; stairs uncarpeted; one cycle, a woman's, propped against the wall; one battered pushchair; a pile of back copies of *Spare Rib*. There was no sign of those small touches by which men create a feeling of home: no golf clubs, no electric drills, no pink flush of the *Financial Times* or unblushing flesh of the *Sun*, no crate of empties. This was perplexing. Also slightly worrying.

'Why don't you come right in?' a voice demanded. Tom looked up.

A woman was coming down the stairs. All he could see at first were quantities of a light Indian print and an erratic gait. This latter was explained by the absence of one shoe and the fact that she was shaking her head vigorously. There was a whirl of spray, most of which fell upon Tom.

'Sorry,' she said. 'Just washed it. Here, this way.'

She led him down the passage and into a back room. 'Good of you to come. I'm running late. So can't show you round. Just ferret about. Coffee by the sink. Milk on the cellar step. No luxuries like a fridge. Ditto telly, but your mother said you had to work.' She shot him a quick grin. 'Mind the loo. The seat won't stand up. You have to hold it. Else do yourself an injury. Don't have that problem myself. Anything else you want to know?'

Tom took a deep breath. 'I've never done this before. Could you fill me in on the duties?'

'There aren't any, except to be here. She's in bed.'

This did not seem adequate. Conscientiously, he tried

to equip himself with background information. 'Does she walk?'

'Walk? Where've you been all this time? 'Course she walks! Walked at ten months. Girls often do. More advanced than boys. Read sooner, too. Hadn't you noticed?'

'Not particularly.'

'Well, you wouldn't, would you? Not nice to admit it.'

'You sound like my mother.'

'Thanks. I mean that. She's all right. What you got against her?'

'How much time have you got?'

She laughed. 'See who you take after.'

'I don't!' The woman's conversational style was catching.

'I mean your dad.'

'You know my dad?'

'Why not? Everybody knows everybody else round here, don't they?' She was on her knees, looking under chairs. 'Seen my sandal?'

'It's on your foot.'

'That's this one.'

'It could be the other.'

'Stop being so funny and have a look.'

They scrambled about on the floor and found it under a discarded nappy.

'Hell, you can see I don't go in for much cleaning. Look at your knees,' she exclaimed, more critical than apologetic.

Fully shod and at the door, she called, 'All right up to eleven or half past?'

Tom shouted agreement, then suddenly panic-stricken, rushed after her. 'What do I do if she wakes?'

'Who? Oh, Sarah. Don't know. She never does. She's a lovely baby. She'll sleep through. Guaranteed.'

The door slammed behind her. Two minutes later a small child stood in the hallway. 'Drink,' she said.

Chapter Two

Next morning Tom woke exhausted. Sleep had not refreshed him and he felt no urge to break the habit of seventeen years by leaping out of bed to greet the new day.

It had been a strenuous evening. Sarah was a thirsty baby and suffered from a condition which prevented her from imbibing more than an ounce at a time. He could sympathize with the problem but deplored the cure: two sips, a brief nap of fifteen minutes, then another trip downstairs. He calculated that he had risen from his books, poured milk, and walked up and down stairs fourteen times. It was a hard way to earn a couple of quid. Which, incidentally, had not yet been received.

But that was not the only reason for his present fatigue. The evening with Sarah had been nothing compared with the night spent pursuing a gauzy dress sprouting daffodils, galloping after a pair of high boots, and engaging in bruising rounds with Tarzan Turnbull. Dozing, he was again striding after her, down the corridor, into the staff room, out to the Science block, into a lab where she paused behind a computer which kept flashing PIN up on its screen. He tried to adopt its advice and pin her in a corner but as he reached her a pair of hairy hands came between them; she turned, and he saw that she was dressed only in a drifting smoke of hair.

Tom slid out of bed and crawled round the floor

looking for his socks. His hands shook as he put them on. Up to now, women had been an optional extra in his life, not one of the basics – loafing around, eating, writing scurrilous articles (unpublished) for the local rag, turning up at school, debating with Dave. But the effect of Miss Faulkner was alarming. It was like nothing he had experienced before, except, he admitted wryly, the first time he had tried to ride a bicycle. He could still remember the fear, exhilaration and sensation of being carried along by a force he could not control.

In an attempt to calm himself, he prepared another unprintable report for the *Moorman Weekly*.

'Virgin(?) Schoolboy's Night of Madness.

'On-the-spot-news.

'People in this quiet north-country town nestling under the lee of the barren moor were still reeling from the shock today after disclosures that a schoolboy (17) and a Physics mistress (25)' – How old was she? – 'had disappeared in the early hours of yesterday morning. "I still can't believe it," wept curly-haired Rugby Blue six-footer Science master Clifford Turnbull (32), as he surveyed the evidence. "It beats me," Sergeant Todd commented, adding, "Though I had a fair bit on the moor myself when I was a lad." Mr John Gordon (45), Headmaster, was not available for comment but there is speculation about second-in-command Mr Childe, known as Nanny to his Sixth. As he left the Sixth Form Centre, a broken man, he was overheard to say, "I am deeply shocked. Taylor was a school prefect and I trusted him to set a better example." '

Feeling better, Tom picked up the shirt he had been wearing the last few days. After a diagnostic sniff, he decided to relinquish it and fetched another from his drawer. A note was pinned to the lapel: 'Top button

16

came off in the wash,' his mother had written. 'Carefully retrieved and placed in pocket. Thread to match bought and in the sewing box downstairs.'

Tom sighed, unpinned the note and added it to his collection of original documents for use in his autobiography. He already had the first sentence. It was a slight refashioning of one from Jane Austen.

He had discovered it three years earlier when Olly Hardy, in a courageous attempt to civilize the boys in his English class, had introduced them to *Northanger Abbey*. Tom had come across the sentence in paragraph three and from then on much of the novel was lost to him. 'From fifteen to seventeen Catherine Morland was in training for a heroine,' he read. The words had struck a chord. A little altered, they stated his servitude.

'You see this,' he had said to Dave. Emotion had made him sweat. Stickily he boxed the sentence round with thick lead. 'Well, I can do better than that. Want to hear? "From eleven to fourteen Tom Taylor was in training for a husband." '

'But you've never been gone on girls!'

'No, not them! It's my mother.'

Dave had been appalled. 'That's not allowed,' he said.

The sentence had lost something in the explanation which followed, but it regained its original glow in private and was updated with each succeeding birthday. Tom said it aloud now, as he drew the edges of his collar together with his tie. 'From eleven to seventeen Tom Taylor was in training for a husband.'

Not, of course, from choice. By imposition. Of his mother.

Suddenly inspired, Tom began to improvise. 'She had come upon the Women's Liberation Movement rather late, thus by default allowing him eleven carefree years. Acknowledging that, by a regrettable mischance, the child she had spawned would never stand in the front ranks of the Cause, i.e. he was male, she nevertheless determined to make good her error in a way which only her defective ingenuity could have devised. That was to prepare him for union with a liberated consort, i.e. woman. To this end, even as a youth barely weaned from his primary school, he was expected to take part in household chores: drying dishes, putting out empty milk bottles, feeding the cat (soon defunct), and such wearisome tasks. As the years passed, the training became more onerous and included learning to cook ghastly dishes of her own creation, cleaning his bedroom and mending his clothes. Being a sweet-tempered lad he was prepared to undertake some of the more creative jobs occasionally, but his objection to her system never faltered because it was based on an outrageous error of logic which she refused to admit. This was: given that this unpaid labour was a necessary training for marriage, how could it be justified if he did not intend to enter that shackled state?'

Tom stopped. The breathing had leapt out of control again. This talk of marriage had brought on the Miss Faulkner syndrome. 'Who ever lov'd that lov'd not at first sight?' Where did that come from? All that hair, that extraordinary cape of hair! He wondered what it was like to touch. Meditating, he rummaged in a drawer, found a brush and set to work.

He admired the effect when he had finished and, leaving home early, was careful to take a route past the laboratories on his way into school. No flare from a Bunsen burner signalled appreciation of his effort, but in the Sixth Form Centre it did not go ignored.

'I like the new hairstyle,' one of the girls said.

18

Kate Morrison asked, 'What's happened to the absent-minded professor bit?'

'Still there, even to the missing button.' Tom fingered his collar and swept the group with practised eye. 'At least, it's not missing, just absent from its place. My laundress left it in the pocket.'

'Then you can sew it back, can't you?' she answered.

But the target for his remarks predictably obliged. 'I'll do it,' Betty said, and dug in her bag for the needlecase and cotton which were an indispensable part of her equipment.

Tom removed his tie, unfastened his shirt and homed in.

'You're not going to let him let you!' Kate exclaimed.

'It won't take a minute.' Betty was a buxom, affectionate girl and, concentrating on the stitches, she pressed close in a businesslike fashion. ('Don't you realize that you are flogging a dead horse?' Tom would sometimes ask his mother. 'Most girls don't *want* to be liberated.')

Finished, pushing herself away from him, she blushed at his thanks and he was tempted to kiss the top of her newly washed hair. (What was Miss Faulkner doing to him?) He saw that Kate still watched, glowering.

However, he could spare no time to think about that. Except for the occasional intrusion of staff denied his full attention, his thoughts that morning were devoted to advancing his acquaintance with Miss Faulkner.

'Hello, fancy bumping into you again!' he rehearsed to himself as, the bell for lunch still ringing, he hurried towards the Science block. Then he would turn casually and walk back with her, inviting her out to a pub lunch. (Seeing whom he escorted, none of the local publicans – who were either law-abiding zealots or school

19

governors – would question his age.) The important thing for a start was that meeting her should appear natural, completely spontaneous.

'Hello, Tom. Don't often see you in these parts. Hanging about for someone?' Stan Driffield greeted, coming out of his woodwork room.

'No; just passing.'

Stan looked down the corridor, puzzled how a journey from the Arts department could be so described. For a moment his eyes rested on the entrance to the Physics labs. 'In that case, I'll join you. I'm going down to lunch myself,' he said, and Tom could find no excuse to remain.

Busily trying to cover the other's embarrassment, Stan said, 'You know what happened to me this morning? Ellard Richardson. You know him? Yes? Remedial! That's the biggest joke in town. He's that because it suits him. Never misses a trick. Today he asked me if he could take the wood shavings for his sister's hamster. I never thought to ask, which sister, which hamster. Haven't time for detailed interrogation with that lot. I could hear him and his mate planing away but didn't interrupt – I'd fifteen less industrious claiming my attention. Then I noticed he scarpered pretty quick after the bell. No wonder. He'd got through about ten quids' worth of wood! Sold as shavings to gullible juniors, it will bring in a fair return for the sweat. Can't wait to get my hands on the little devil.'

'I'd like to see that,' Tom said, negligently, and caught the other's swift glance. He blushed, sorry for his rebuff. He liked Stan Driffield. The man did not demand pupils' deference, nor did he assume a right to probe into private thoughts.

Instead, queuing in the canteen, he said easily, 'How's

20

Mike? Looked tired last time I saw him. I offered to swap jobs for a bit. Wouldn't mind trying my hand at management consultancy, but I don't reckon his talents much in practical woodwork, do you?'

'Not much,' Tom agreed, his eyes raking the tables.

'It must be over a month since I had a jar with him. He having another spell of work away?' Stan persisted.

'That's right.' Tom found it difficult to simulate interest in his father's occupation and movements, faced with an empty canteen. That is, apart from several hundred people gorging themselves on reeking cabbage, it was empty. She was not there. No doubt Cliff Turnbull had carried her off again, he told himself, aiming at total depression. He had probably got her over a sandwich in some low dive in town. Not that the town sported any low dives, but any place was transformed into one by Tarzan's presence. Without much success, he tried to concentrate on selecting from the plates ranged along the counter in front of him.

'You on a diet?' Stan asked. His own tray was liberally piled. 'Wait till school lunch is the only meal you don't prepare for yourself.'

'It often is.'

Stan smiled, disbelieving.

They looked round for an empty table. By custom, those near the door were reserved for staff, but, encouraged by the headmaster, the more egalitarian would often mingle with the mob, serenely ignoring the dismay they caused. Tom saw Roland Goodenough, the Social Studies man, sitting alone flanked by tables of babbling pupils. Mournful but conscientious, he waited patiently for problems to offer themselves for solution. Automatically, Stan and Tom walked to another part of the canteen.

'And how's Belinda? Haven't seen her for some time, either. Summer holidays, I suppose.'

'Yes. They keep her out of the way a bit.'

Stan looked blank. 'Well, yes. Incidentally, about that sink unit she was having fitted. There's no need for her to fetch a man in, you know. I'll see to it for her.' Stan lifted the crust of his meat pie and examined the contents eagerly.

'I think it's been done.'

'A pity about that.' He gazed at the slice of pie impaled on the tines of his fork. It appeared to have lost its attraction. Then, brightening, he added, 'Still, there's a book I must return to her. I'll drop in with it some time.'

'I'll take it for you,' Tom said, prepared to protect the man from unnecessary exposure to his mother, but the offer was refused. Clearly Stan had a tendency to masochism, but at the moment Tom had no inclination to conduct a session of psychological analysis.

Attempting to sound casual, he remarked, 'I keep seeing new faces. I expect there must be a number of new staff.'

'Yes, but not many. The turnover is not high. People know when they're on to a good thing, not much hassle. It's very different here from a big inner-city school.'

'What are they like – the new staff?'

'The usual mix.' Stan shovelled rice pudding into his mouth and looked at him, calculating.

Go on, curse you, Tom said silently. You found me outside the Physics labs. You can guess what I want to know. 'Some more mixed than others, I suppose,' he muttered, feeling defeated.

'Well, they're mostly young and lively and seem to have plenty of interests.' He paused, watching Tom's face. At last he said, 'For example, there's a new Physics woman who's already signed up for staff hockey, goes in for fell walking, and has done a lot in amateur theatre.'

'Never a dull moment,' Tom murmured.

Outdoor sports and acting! Why was she not interested in things he could do? He compiled a list, then discarded it. It was a sad business, totting up the details of a wasted youth.

Stan rose. 'I'll have to go. There's a meeting at one o'clock.' Then, with his eyes avoiding Tom's face, he added, 'And, just for the record, she's called Faulkner. Jonquil Faulkner.'

Jonquil. Tom remained in the canteen, repeating her name softly to himself, while his rice pudding congealed upon his plate.

Jonquil. He wrote it later in the margin of his French dictation and considered its shape. A beautiful name, apt for the one who possessed it. Better than daffodils, more dainty. He scribbled his own beside it: Tom. It was unsatisfactory, ordinary, unheroic. He needed a new image. Altered to Thomas, it was much improved, a good title with some remarkable holders: Thomas Becket, Thomas Jefferson, Thomas Carlyle, Thomas Babbington Macaulay, Doubting Thomas. He added a few curlicues before scratching it all out and returning to the dictation. It occurred to him that he was lapsing into an infantile state.

The same notion troubled the French teacher that evening when, confused by omissions, she held the paper to the light and deciphered, Thomas Stearns Eliot, a signature which failed to compensate for the lines she sought.

However, by the time the French lesson was over,

Tom had decided that the charm of Jonquil's name was no substitute for the woman in the flesh. The phrase started the raucous breathing again, and Tom looked round anxiously, checking whether anyone had heard. He would soon have a reputation: Tom Taylor, the original heavy breather, on his way to a telephone kiosk and a quick fix. But failing immediate access to that, he walked towards the Science block. A visit there seemed the best way to spend a free period. If he could not manage to speak to her, at least he could get near.

Reaching his observation point, a crate of mutilated equipment awaiting disposal, he levered himself up and looked through the glass. She was not there. Instead, there was another face not ten inches from his own. It stayed there, too, in spite of some unambiguous encouragement to move, and it drew closer, going in for frantic lip movements and sprouting an arm on the end of which was a hand which grabbed the latch of the window. This swung out, caught Tom on the shoulder and swept him off his perch.

'What the hell do you think you're playing at?' Cliff Turnbull shouted through the hole. 'Keep away from these labs or I'll have you up for loitering with intent.'

'And I'll have you up for assault,' Tom shouted back, nursing his shoulder. 'An unprovoked attack, that was. Look good on the billboards: Physics Master Assaults Boy on School Premises. Pervert's Post-Prandial Sin.'

'Clear off, you bloody Arts git. You've no business to be round here,' and the window banged shut.

Tom thought it better not to argue the point.

But the incident was invigorating. That curly-haired stand-in for Tarzan had been bothering him all day because he had everything in his favour: reputation, experience, age, and on-the-spot opportunity. But that did not mean that he, Tom, was beaten. He would find some way. On an impulse he left the path back to the Sixth Form Centre, crossed the car park and entered the main building.

'I wonder if I could have Miss Faulkner's address,' he said to a secretary.

She dragged her attention from her machine and looked up. 'Miss Faulkner's home address?'

'That's right.'

'You mean where she's living?'

'Yes.' He wondered whether flash cards would help her.

'I'm not allowed to hand out staff addresses without reason. They are confidential.'

'But there's no secret where staff live. They would have a hard job to conceal their bolt-holes in this town.'

'Those are my orders.'

Tom bit back abuse and opted for subterfuge. 'She's left early, to go to the dentist, so has asked me to deliver some books, but unfortunately she forgot to give her address.'

'What's your name?'

There was no need for a false beard and moustache in front of the school secretaries. They kept their heads down in the corridors and had no wish to match faces to names in their files. 'Reginald Grimshaw,' Tom answered, hoping it would not be necessary to confess to R.G.

'Marjorie, give this boy Miss Faulkner's address, will you? And book her as having had a dental appointment this afternoon. I'll check with her later. It's always wise to check.' She looked at Tom and bared her dentures in a satisfied grimace. He stumbled out, but anxiety about what he might have set in motion was dispelled by the slip of paper in his hand.

The true R.G., untroubled by knowledge of Tom's impersonation, drew up beside him as he walked down the school drive.

Rolling down the window, he invited, 'Like a lift? Help yourself.'

Tom attempted to help himself to the front seat, discovered a languid form already there, so added his bulk to the back where conditions were more cramped.

They were talking about university applications. 'You didn't come to Nanny's meeting this lunch hour,' Kate said from somewhere underneath him. 'He was going over entrance requirements, and your absence did not go unnoticed.'

'I forgot. I had other things on my mind.'

'Lucky you. Anyway, I collected your UCCA form.'

'Thanks.' Though filling that in was well down his list of priorities.

'My parents are insisting I apply,' Julia of the front seat was complaining. 'Drama school's out. All they'll concede is a course combining some drama that gives a teaching qualification so that I have that to fall back on. Imagine me falling back on teaching!'

'Imagine teaching after you've fallen back on it. I'll work out the equation,' Pin said.

'It's all right for you! Nobody stops you littering everywhere with useless machines, whereas my father won't even let me be in a play this year. Says I've got to get decent A-levels, so he refuses to allow me to audition for the autumn season at Gritley Thespians. And their shows are reviewed in the *Yorkshire Post*.'

'I know a guy who works on the *Yorkshire Post*,' R.G. said, trying to be helpful. Then, to curtail Julia's flow of sardonic abuse, he added, 'The boss my end is digging his heels in, as well. Use of car no more than twice a week, home by midnight, and half-pay up to the November retakes. Been going on about having a moron for a son and four tries for O-level English can no longer be explained by the inability of examiners to recognize my latent literacy. I say to him, you never took an exam in your life and look where it got you, and he says the days of pulling yourself up by your bootstraps are over, and that I don't have the muscle or brain for that anyway.'

'I don't understand why you can't pass it,' Kate told him. 'You must have a block about it by now. I'll give you a hand if you like.'

'Thanks, Kate, you're on,' he shouted back to her. 'How much an hour?' However unsatisfactory, R.G. remained his father's son.

The school grind, Julia's father, R.G.'s cash-flow (to be summarily cut off if he failed English language again), Dave's latest story (returned), Kate's complaints that the town offered no alternative to homework (except flower arranging, bell ringing, Spanish for package holidays and weight watching at the Further Education Centre) and the obstacles in the way of under-age drinking (from Pin) continued to occupy them, but Tom made no contribution. Nor was he influenced by the subsequent gloom. His thoughts were taken up with an address on the paper he stroked in his pocket, and with the enchanting sound of her name.

Reaching home, he found a note which directed him to a pork chop in the refrigerator and suggested that he prepare himself a salad to accompany it. He examined the uncooked chop, replaced it and cracked a couple of eggs into a frying pan. As these congealed, he added a tin of baked beans in which nestled five anaemic cylinders alleged to be sausages, a segment of Camembert cheese and a tin of condensed mushroom soup. Stirring fused the ingredients into a homogeneous mess for which the only appropriate music was Radio One. He moved the volume button just short of where the transistor would explode and ate the concoction straight from the pan.

When he had finished, he found his pen and reported back to his mother: 'I did not feel up to any intensive cooking this evening so I made myself a light sandwich and took an aspirin with a glass of milk. I intend to go to bed early, so please do not disturb if /when you return.' Pinning the note on the board beside the calendar, he compared the engagements and reflected upon the unequal distribution. His mother's column was a dense pattern of times, pursuits and vigorous calls to action: 'P. wants that report by now' and 'Find exam papers for class.' Mike was more reticent; he shaded in the periods he was away and drew a star on the days he was at home. Tom liked the symbolism and thought it might be worth imitating, so he sketched a sun on the days in his column and added a key: 'Will be in for breakfast and supper.' He wrote 'School' on several days and then gave up. There are details unsuitable for recording on a kitchen calendar. After that, he took the *Guardian* into the lavatory and read for a comfortable half hour until considerations of scholarship obliged him to examine alternative expressions of Manchester culture, and he went downstairs to watch 'Coronation Street'. Lacking a detailed summary of the action over the last twenty years, he found the plot difficult to follow but wondered whether Yorkshire Television might be interested in a series he and Dave could run up, something on the lines of 'Life is the Blanks on the Kitchen Calendar Waiting to be Filled In.'

And it was time, at last, to fill in one of them. She would be there by now, fed and rested after an arduous day evading the embrace of Tarzan. There was no longer excuse for delay. Tom smoothed his hair in front of a mirror, told himself that his pallor was the result of autosuggestion after his mention of the aspirin and, checking that he had the address, he left the house.

Chapter Three

After a short distance on the level it was a steady climb
to the place he sought, but the physical exertion could
not explain his feeling of weakness or the block of ice
lodged inside his stomach, so he attempted some
emergency therapy by reciting: nothing venture, nothing win; fortune favours the bold; he who hesitates is
lost – and similar mindless maxims. Unfortunately,
they were no help and he was sweating and unsteady
by the time he reached her road.

It was the last of those running at right angles to the
steep approach to the moor, following the contour lines
with a few undulations. The houses were large, durable,
fashioned from millstone grit by Victorian wool men,
and the address on Tom's paper was of one which had
been converted into flats. There was a drive flanked by
rhododendrons, excellent cover for snipers, Tom noted;
a flight of steps guarded by stone beasts, much eroded
but still fully fanged; then the door, huge, wooden,
hinged with iron and decorated with black studs.

Tom leant against the arch in which it was set,
wondering at the foolishness which had brought him
there. He had no plan. He had no idea what he could
say. He had no reason to give for his visit. Except the
simple one he could not divulge: that he wanted to
speak to her, hear her voice, see her close. He looked
down the steps, over the rhododendrons, the road, and
the few spires and chimneys which were the only

evidence of the town hidden by the drop of the land. Behind him was the door. It was impossible to escape it. He turned, pushed it abruptly and entered the porch. Before this spurt of courage flickered out, Tom strode across to a panel of buttons, found the one labelled: Flat Four, Jonquil Faulkner, and pressed.

Waiting, he heard the scrape of his breath, listened to the sound of her name typed and kept clean under a plastic shield; observed the scrubbed mosaic at his feet; felt his tongue draw across dry lips and his mind scrabbling for words he must discover. Then something crackled and a voice above him, distinct but distant, asked who was there.

Shocked, unprepared for this, Tom jumped back, noticed for the first time the grilles, wires and paraphernalia for contact, and his resolution broke.

'Hello, who is it?' the voice demanded again, businesslike, a little irritated. 'Have you rung the right bell?'

Tom edged a step towards the grille, drew breath and whispered into its metallic ear, 'Sorry. A mistake.' Then fled.

'So that was it,' he explained to Sarah. 'I scarpered. I just couldn't say my name into that damned contraption. I was, as the old cliché has it, at a loss for words. Now that probably wouldn't bother you much; you get along nicely without many, but I need them. I'm hooked on words, one of the disadvantages of growing old.'

Sarah nibbled her biscuit and considered his disability.

They were in the kitchen, Tom leaning against the draining board and Sarah perched on top of the cooker, the only piece of furniture which did not fold or sag at a touch.

'I shot down the drive, back along the road, ignoring the speed limit, and rattled up the path on to the moor. When I reached the trees below Nether Gill I paused for a while, I don't know how long, my breast bursting, as the saying goes, with unsuppressible emotion, until I realized that I was standing directly above her flat. But that position, my innocent little Sarah, was not near enough, so I cut straight down till I was about twenty yards outside the back garden, selected a convenient boulder, and settled down to watch. Yes, I can't deny it. I squatted there in the semi-darkness, my vigil lit by a few rather low-watt stars, and watched, thinking perhaps she would come to a window, close a curtain or something. I wasn't hoping for anything sensational, just a glimpse.'

'Juice,' Sarah interrupted.

'It's milk, my dear. M-I-L-K,' he spelt out, waving the bottle.

She shook her head. 'Juice,' she insisted. Then, tutting, she rotated on her buttocks, lay across the cooker and, wriggling her stomach over the edge, slid down. When she reached the floor, she pulled her nightgown into place and staggered across the room. The storage arrangements in the kitchen were simple: pans and crockery were kept on the draining board or under foam in the sink according to the point they had reached in the cycle of use; food was in cardboard cartons ranged along the floor. With an accuracy derived from constant practice, Sarah located the orange juice.

'Oh, I see. Clever girl,' Tom complimented her.

She regarded him complacently and accepted a measure without thanks. He joined her on the floor.

'I haven't told you everything about the evening. You

see, I was disturbed. Someone came upon me. At first, it was only a dog.'

'Dog!' She swivelled to look behind her, slopping some of the juice.

'No, not here,' he soothed, and wiped her dry with the hem of her nightgown. 'Don't get nervous. I haven't brought one. This . . .'

He paused. Sarah waited, apprehensive. He would have to employ a synonym. Luckily there were plenty. 'Look, I was crouched there and this came sniffing round, this cur, bitch, bobtail tyke, pup, hound, whelp, mongrel.' Sarah was looking more relaxed. 'You like that one, do you? Mongrel. A mongrel called Moloch.'

She giggled, so he repeated the sentence several times while she rocked on her bottom enthusiastically and sprayed juice over herself like a drunk.

Tom found her appreciation stimulating.

'Moloch is a mongrel that mongrels on the moor,' he chanted. 'He mongrels and he mongrels till his Moloch paws be sore.'

Sarah was convulsed.

'I'll show you how he mongrels, here upon the floor.'

He got to his knees, shook himself, scratched, whined gently, sniffed round her and licked her glass. She raised it tipsily and poured the remaining drops down his chin.

'And he masticates his orange juice inside his Moloch maw.'

'More,' Sarah echoed, and proffered her empty glass.

'You like your tipple, don't you, old girl? I think I'll join you.'

When they were settled opposite each other again, flushed but calmer, Tom said, 'Right. That's the end of the funny stuff. Now for the serious bit. Because this beastie, having peed liberally on a pile of harmless rocks, flopped at my feet and sent up a volley of barks. And can you guess who appeared? Stan Driffield. I can admit to you I was embarrassed. Walking on the moor in the evening, especially with the excuse of a beastie, is all right, but just sitting on it looks rather odd. Stan seemed uncomfortable, too.

‘ "You don't mind?" he asked as he lowered himself beside me.

‘ "Of course not. Help yourself," I said.

‘We attempted chat, but it was strained.

‘He said, "Waiting for someone?"

‘I said, "Sort of."

‘He said, "Like that, is it?"

‘And I said, "Yes!" ’

Sarah wriggled impatiently. She was developing a tic, blinking jerkily and rubbing her lids.

‘Stan pulled at the grass and I could hear him chewing on a blade as if it were his first meal of the day. Then he said, "The new Physics woman, Jonquil Faulkner, lives down there. Her garden backs on to the moor, but I've never seen her out when I've been taking a turn with the beastie."

‘He knew, of course, and I couldn't say anything. But not because I wanted to snub him. It was something else that kept me quiet. Something weird. (Wake up, girl, you're falling asleep.) It was as if he knew how I was feeling because he'd had it himself. The disease, I mean, you fathead. (Concentrate when I'm talking to you.) Or still had. He's not that old.

‘After a while he said, "Just looked in at your place, Tom. Nobody there. I'll try another time when I'm airing the hound."

‘ "Belinda doesn't much care for them."

' "Thanks. I'll remember that." He seemed grateful for the information. "Well, I'll leave you. It's getting cold. Thanks for the advice about the hound," he repeated and, as if he were offering something in exchange, added, "She, Jonquil Faulkner, has joined Gritley Thespians for their November production. No doubt a lot of her spare time will be taken up."

'He went, and I gave him ten minutes' start before following him down the path.'

During the last part of the narrative, Sarah had been standing by his shoulder. This position brought her face on a level with his.

'So, I've told you all,' he said, poking a finger above her ear where hairs were gummed together by juice. 'I don't know whether you have anything to say about it.'

She nodded, leant to him and whispered, 'Wee.'

Tom pushed himself up. 'Well, I suppose that's fair comment,' he said.

The next three hours should have been devoted to Bismarck, but he failed to compel. After thirty minutes Tom gave up. Much of the last fortnight had been spent reliving each ghastly moment of his visit but he had not dwelt on his talk with Stan. That had been too embarrassing. Tonight, however, encouraged by Sarah, he had narrated it all. Again, Stan's farewell came back to him. It was brief, unsolicited, but suddenly relevant, bulging with possibilities: Jonquil Faulkner has joined Gritley Thespians for their November production.

That is the answer, Tom told himself, Gritley Thespians. There he could meet her in the most natural way.

He would play opposite her, light her cigarette, pour her a drink, catch her as she fainted, carry her to a sofa, chafe her hands. These scenes provoked enjoyable sensations but also raised, Tom had to

35

admit, a couple of difficulties. One was that few plays nowadays were written with those requirements in mind, and the other was that he had never set foot on the boards and it might be hard to persuade the Gritley lot to give him his first break in a principal role. Yet he felt certain that here lay his chance and there was a hint somewhere of how he could manage it. It involved Julia Marshall.

Tom fetched a glass of orange juice, removed his shoes, collected pen and paper and focussed thought with a few notes.

1. Stan says Jonquil has joined the Grit. Thes. for Nov. production.
2. No reason why I should not join, too.
3. But this may look suspicious since never shown interest before.
4. Need an excuse. Julia Marshall.
5. Her parents refusing to let her take part, because of A-levels.
6. Must find a way to get round that.

Tom lay back on the hearthrug and read through the notes. He found them encouraging but the exercise had exhausted him.

Since he had first seen that wimple of gleaming hair and the flounced voile furled round immaculate boots in the corridor's draught, he had vacillated between states of nervous expectation and fatigue. He flipped *The Mayor of Casterbridge* off the chair with a foot, turned on his side and started to read. He was beginning to relate to Henchard's difficulties in contacting Lucetta.

A foot in his ribs disturbed his dreams. 'My Gawd, you can snore,' its owner said.

Tom looked up a pair of well-moulded legs. There was a good deal above, from which he considered it seemly to avert his eyes. He blew the skirt aside and scrambled on to the sofa. 'I've had a hard day.'

'I bet.' Liz sniggered. 'Bring her here. I don't mind.'

'Her? Oh, I see. Unfortunately, that's not possible.'

'Lives away, does she?'

'No, but she hasn't exactly succumbed to my charms.'

'Like that, is it? I should pack that in.' She rolled on to the sofa and sat beside him. 'Plenty more fish on the beach.'

'In the sea,' he corrected conscientiously.

'As far as I'm concerned, on the beach. They're all washed up by the time they reach me.'

'I'm sorry,' he answered, caught her expression and they both laughed.

'You should have been at the Dalesway. Singles' Evening.'

Tom tried to sort that out.

'Really one-parent families.'

'That seems a contradiction in terms,' he hedged.

'Clever Dick. It's if you're divorced. Or separated. Or an unmarried mother.'

'I didn't know,' he mumbled and gestured feebly in her direction.

'Hasn't Belinda said? Tactful, but not necessary.'

'I wouldn't put tact very high on her list of propensities.'

'You're prejudiced. You've got at her before. Anyway, it's not a secret. You can't keep much secret round here, can you? I'm surprised you didn't know. Where've you been all this time?'

'You've asked me that before.'

'Well, you give that impression. Not quite in the picture.'

'I'm sorry. Suppose you put me in this one.'

37

'You making a proposition? Oh, all right. Skip it. It's a cheat really, me going to the Singles' Evening. Because there's Don. Occasionally. When he bothers. He's a half-timer. But I reckon he'll soon knock off for keeps.' This speech tired her and the effort to sustain it required her to lean against his arm. Her hair was the same colour as Sarah's and it, too, bore a few matted knots at the edges. Tom resisted the urge to poke his fingers through them and straighten them out.

'Mind you, there are compensations,' she added. 'Freedom, for one.'

'Such as Singles' Night at the Dalesway?' He was distracted by the weight on his arm.

'Don't be sarcastic! That's more of an insurance.'

'But you wouldn't have freedom if you married again.'

'Who's talking about marriage?'

'Oh, I see.'

'About time. And, thank Gawd, I don't depend on the Dalesway.'

'I'm pleased to hear that.' Wedged between them, his hand had gone numb.

'Because there aren't many eligible men there. When you look round.'

'Eligible for what?'

She leant forward, cackling like a maniac. It seemed he had a similar effect on the mother as on the daughter. Such appreciation was good for his ego. He grinned at her while flapping his released hand to aid resuscitation.

'What's wrong with you? Bad circulation?'

'A form of manual communication.'

'You'll have to make it clearer. Can't make it out,' she said, and began to move back.

He judged it was the moment to suggest a break. 'Can I get you a cup of coffee? Or juice?'

'Juice?' The word itself was sobering.

'I know where it is. Sarah showed me. We had a quiet drink and a chat together.'

'A chat? With Sarah?'

'You do have to supply the odd word when she is at a loss, but that's no problem. She seems interested in poetry.'

'You're having me on! But I'm sorry. She shouldn't have bothered you. I said not to come down again.'

'Don't worry about it,' then stopped, hearing her last word. 'How do you mean, again?'

'Like last time, of course.'

'But I didn't tell you.'

'Her next door said.'

'How did she know?'

'Jawing at the gate most of the evening, and the curtains weren't drawn.'

'Hadn't she anything better to do than watch what was going on?'

Liz raised an eyebrow. ' 'Course not. It's her hobby. Like most folks's round here. Why so steamed up? It's no matter.'

'I suppose not.' But the news depressed him. He felt as if something intimate had been exposed, chatted about, passed round for comment. With a jerk of dismay he connected this gossip to Jonquil Faulkner. If his experience with Sarah was worthy of mention, what would they make of his pursuit of a teacher? And the sensation that provided would not be confined to people in the town; there were the kids in school and the gaggle of prurient staff. He cursed silently as he collected his books. He would have to be careful. He could not bear anyone to know how he felt.

'I'll be going,' he announced unnecessarily.

She followed him into the hall and propped herself against the half-opened door. Tom felt that some kind of farewell was required but he could think of nothing appropriate.

'Pleased you enjoyed the Singles' Evening,' he tried.

She grinned, slanting her head. 'Beggars can't be losers.'

'Choosers.'

'No, losers. Think about it, you daft ha'p'orth,' and she bobbed forward and kissed him on the cheek.

Chapter Four

'There is no reason why her parents should know,' Tom argued.

'Word is bound to get round,' Kate said.

Dave was more helpful. 'But it's in Gritley, not here. That's eight miles away. It isn't likely to hit the headlines of the *Moron Weekly*.'

'It carries advertisements for the Thespian productions,' Kate pointed out.

'Only the week before performances,' Tom said.

'By which time, *fait accompli*,' Pin commented, explaining, 'This week I'm into French.'

'But even if they aren't alerted by the *Moorman*, I can't see how she can prevent her parents from knowing,' Kate insisted.

Tom glared at her. He could not understand why she was making so many objections. It was nearly a week since his resolution to meet Jonquil at Gritley Thespians by persuading Julia to audition for the November production. Every time he had tried to suggest she did so, something else had intervened. It was particularly irritating to meet Kate's opposition now that he had finally manoeuvred the discussion as far as this.

Kate continued, 'She has to go to rehearsals. They can hardly not notice. Wouldn't your parents?'

'The question is not relevant,' Tom answered. 'My parents are rarely there themselves.'

'Oh, what a shame!' Betty's sympathy was genuine. 'What do you do?'

'I manage.' He smiled bravely. Betty looked disappointed. Clearly, sewing on the occasional button did not satisfy her maternal craving. He must remember to bring his orange sweater; he rather fancied it jazzed up with a few decorative patches.

Ignoring Kate's eye, he continued, 'We could think up plenty of excuses. Julia could say she was spending the time with one of us, working or something, that I was giving her a hand. I don't mind,' he urged.

'They might. They might even prefer her at the theatre,' Kate said.

'Do you really think I ought to try it, Tom?' Julia appealed.

'I do. What we have to concentrate on first, though, is getting you to the audition.' He had no wish to be encumbered with Julia indefinitely. All he needed was the excuse to be there once, then he could allow himself to be persuaded to help. These amateur groups were always anxious to engage labour of the unapplauded sort.

'As a matter of fact, I've already been invited. It's as if you knew, Tom,' she whispered soulfully, resting a hand on his arm.

'What's the play?' Kate's question was loud.

'A Taste of Honey. They want me for Jo, of course. And what a part!'

The others agreed. If Julia were to gain notice, there could be no better opportunity.

'I saw the film once,' Pin said. 'Is Jo the mother or the daughter?'

Julia glowered. 'The daughter, naturally. You're not suggesting I could play a forty-year-old tart, are you?'

'You could have a go. Where's your sense of challenge?'

'Jo will be challenging enough. I'll wait till I'm past it before I start taking parts like Helen.'

'Is that the mother's name? I don't remember that, but I do remember other things about her.' Pin leered round.

'And I'll make damn sure you remember my Jo,' Julia snapped.

So Jonquil must be producing it, Tom thought. Obviously she could not take Helen and there was no other woman in the play.

'They definitely want me,' Julia was repeating. 'The message came by Stan Driffield.'

'Stan?' Tom asked.

'Yes. You know, he builds sets for them occasionally? He's doing the one for *A Taste of Honey*.'

That explained how Stan knew Jonquil's intentions. Previously, in scattered moments given to the subject, Tom had assumed the information derived from staff-room chat. Then suddenly he made the connection. No wonder the man knew all about her. No wonder he had offered to build the set for her production. No wonder he pretended to exercise his dog while roaming the moor behind her flat. He, too, wanted her. Stan!

This was worse than having Tarzan for a competitor. It was like entering for a prize that you would like the other fellow to win. But Stan did not seem very confident. He had the disease, all right, but he had not made much progress with the cure. May the best man win, Tom told himself; all's fair in love and war, and other mindless clichés.

It appeared that Julia had asked him a question. 'Of course,' he gushed, enthusiastically. 'Don't you worry about it. We'll get you there. Forget the parent problem. We'll make sure that you're in the play.'

'Oh, Tom!' she breathed, and to his astonishment and, for that matter, the astonishment of the assembled company, Tom found himself with a young woman weeping lavishly against his chest. As he attempted to support her, and even, in an embarrassed fashion, scrub a greasy handkerchief over her face, some instinct caused him to glance up. Kate had left the group and was already at the door. She turned; their eyes met. Then she shrugged, made a wry grimace, and walked away.

For a reason he was unable to analyse, Tom wanted to rush after her but it was some time before Julia could be persuaded to remove her weight.

They followed Kate to the main building and stood outside Roland Goodenough's room. Julia had recovered more quickly than might have been expected and she was vivacious, entertaining them with gossip about Gritley Thespians and going in for a lot of flirtatious touching, most of which settled on Tom.

'You've never had a go at acting, though you are interested,' she said to him. 'Why don't you try for one of the young men?'

'I don't think I'm quite suitable,' attempting to disengage fingers clamped over his wrist. 'One is black and the other's gay.'

'What's the problem?' Kate asked.

'Playing a West Indian, I reckon I'd lack a certain authenticity.'

'I was thinking of the other.'

'Thanks,' he smiled amiably, but she continued scowling.

Tom wondered what was wrong with her. She had

been moody ever since the beginning of term, but before he could frame a discreet inquiry such as, 'Why the hell are you bugging me, Kate?' Goodenough's door opened.

They entered after a number of Fifth Formers had scrambled out, both groups hampered by piles of discarded waste. These were Goodenough's Collections Points. There was clothing for Oxfam, blankets and every unthinkable household reject for the battered wives' refuge, milk-bottle tops in plastic laundry bags and stacks of yellowing newspapers, every ton convertible into ten pounds for Save the Whale.

Today, extra clutter was provided by a swollen rucksack on Goodenough's desk, over which Ellard Richardson was haranguing sternly, 'I'm telling you, sir, you won't get a better bargain.'

'But I don't happen to own a hamster, Richardson.'

'No matter. It's just as good for rabbits or guinea-pigs.'

'I haven't any pets.'

'That's bad, sir. Pets is nice. I could easily get you one, only that'd be extra.'

'Really, Richardson! I have no wish for a pet, and no need for woodshavings.'

'You have to see it as an investment, sir, and this is real prime stuff. Look!' He dipped a hand into the sack and pulled out a fistful of coiled slivers. 'No muck, no nasty edges. I'm letting it go to you for 30p a quarter — 25p off four pounds or over.'

'Four pounds! You'd need a small van to take that away.'

'I can arrange that. No trouble.'

'I suppose I should have taken some,' Goodenough confided miserably when Ellard had left. 'I don't like to repulse personal effort, particularly in the lower streams. It is a very real dilemma and perhaps you should consider its inclusion, Kate, in your opening presentation of the module, "Social Responsibilities, Two".

'Now, without further delay, let us proceed with today's symposium but before we do so perhaps I should recapitulate the objectives of these – I prefer not to call them lessons – these dialogues which, as I commented last week, have been reluctantly allowed us, but we mustn't look gift horses in the mouth.' Goodenough laughed, offering his own for inspection. 'We are making no attempt to cover all the topics for syndicate discussion that you missed lower down the school, such as: "School, A Necessary Evil?" "Television, A Blessing or a Curse?" "Crime, Does it Pay?" ' He paused, remembering Ellard Richardson's spirited contribution to the last, after which he had withdrawn it as a subject for class participation and substituted an antiquated film on life in a borstal. 'Instead, we shall concern ourselves with components which have greater developmental potential and an increased life-role relevance as you approach the end of your school careers to begin Life Outside. Taylor, I wonder whether, three weeks today, you would be responsible for Women's Liberation?'

'You can't make him take all the blame, Mr Goodenough,' Pin interrupted.

Puzzled, Roland Goodenough explained, 'It would be a natural bridging unit to our "Race" seminar and I thought Taylor would be familiar with the subject since his mother is quite an expert in the field.'

'She does tinker with some of the ideas,' Tom said. 'Shall I ask her to come and speak to us? I'm sure she would agree.'

'I would prefer you to do it, Taylor.'

Tom smiled sympathetically. 'I understand. But I don't know if I could cover everything. There's an awful lot: the historical angle, Seneca Falls, Marx. Then there are all the different groups: prostitute rights, gay women, bisexualists.'

Goodenough was seen to wince. 'Some may have to be omitted, but I can see we shall be in for some very provocative instruction. Meanwhile, we must begin the forum of the day, "Euthanasia". The floor is yours, Aspinall.'

'Right. I haven't bothered with the usual stuff,' Dave began. 'By now everybody knows about Exit. I thought it would be more interesting to look at some examples of people in favour of euthanasia or, more exactly, states of mind when death is welcomed or seems the only possible course. I had a word with Mr Hardy, and he was very happy to lend us some books. Very good of him to cooperate, don't you think, Mr Goodenough?' Dave fished into his grip and passed the books round. 'Keats. Page sixty-five. *Ode to a Nightingale*.'

'I don't like to interfere when you have given so much thought to this, Aspinall, but I'm not sure . . .'

'You will be when we have read it and I have given a commentary. The lines I particularly want to draw your attention to are in stanza six:

' "Now more than ever seems it rich to die,
    To cease upon the midnight with no pain,
    While thou art pouring forth thy soul abroad
       In such an ecstasy."

Julia, would you read for us?'

'Charmed.'

By the time she had finished, everyone else had selected a poem and the lesson passed in pleasurable reading.

'I liked that,' Tom complimented Dave that evening.

'So did I,' he agreed, stretching out on a lovingly made bed. (It was clear that, unlike Belinda, Mrs Aspinall had a proper notion of her duties towards her son.) 'When Nanny said we had to go to that option – note how options turn out to be compulsory – he said that it would provide general knowledge for entrance papers and interviews. It must have been one of his private jokes. Imagine an Oxford don asking me where I stand on extramarital sex!'

'Are you trying for that?'

'Being single, it's the only sort I can try for.'

'For Oxford.'

'Yes. And Kate. What about you?'

'I hadn't thought about it.'

'You'd better get thinking. The applications have to be in early next month. How do you manage to elude Nanny so effectively?'

'It seems a bit irrelevant at present. I've other things on my mind.'

'You do give that impression.'

'Do I?' Tom hesitated, wanting to confide. Always he and Dave had been frank, had kept nothing back, but this was different; his feelings for Jonquil were not suitable for exposure. Yet to hide them seemed to question Dave's trust. The thought was depressing. 'I've a lot on,' he evaded.

'So I gather. Practically hyperactive. For one thing, there's all this mooching about on the moor. Rumour has it that the place is becoming your new habitat.'

'Who says that?'

Dave shrugged. 'People. I suppose it affords a respite from the labours of babysitting. Or is it just a different kind of exercise? I imagine a shoeless nymph chasing you all evening round the crib, eventually cornering you behind the baby bouncer.'

'It's not a bit like that.'

'No, I don't suppose it is. All the same, it's something, isn't it, whatever it is? It's not exactly secondhand. Written down, it would have the conviction of personal experience, wouldn't it? Not like the sort of thing I think up.'

'What's got into you, Dave?'

'That novel I told you about came back second post today. With a copy of some sadist's report. It seems that, I quote: "The plot is implausible and characters lack depth. This writer relies on many stock assumptions about human behaviour which rob his theme of the seriousness for which he clearly, indeed insistently, aims. Even in the less bizarre episodes and among the less banal characters (if one can make such distinctions), the writing lacks the conviction of personal experience." '

Tom was appalled. 'They wrote that?'

' 'S right, Watson.'

'I think if I had received anything like that, I'd have slit my wrists.'

'That did cross my mind.'

'It's worse than anything Olly Hardy could have dreamed up.' To console, he pointed out, 'But at least they sent a report. It means the script got past the office girl.'

'What do you know about it?'

'Belinda reads typescripts for some sleazy publisher.'

'You never told me that before!'

'I try not to dwell too much on my mother's activities. Look, why don't you ask her to look at a few things? She might be able to help. She knows the field.'

'Do you think she would?'

'She'd love to.' Tom grinned. He liked the arrangement, a good turn for a friend which inconvenienced his mother.

Dave looked much improved.

'And forget that crap about personal experience.' He was arguing away the uneasiness Dave's words had caused. For was not he indulging in dreams instead of getting on with the real thing? 'You have to rely on your imagination. Surely there are things you can perceive, feelings you can have, before you can test them in practice? If you ever get as far as that. You can't experience the lot.'

'I wouldn't mind having a go.' Dave leered. 'Except that there are one or two things I'd draw the line at. Not like you.'

'I'm not with you.'

'Don't act so coy! For the last three weeks, ever since the beginning of term, you've been wandering about like a half-wit – Orlando in every respect, except pinning verses on trees. I was intrigued. Who, I asked myself, is the mind-blasting bird? When I got down to it, there seemed a number of candidates – surprising in view of your previously monkish habits. Top of the bill was your monosyllabic Liz. She'll suit him fine, I thought; no ambition to beat his rhetoric while getting down to the job. I listed a few more, but do you know, I missed the right one? That is, until that little episode today. Tom, why does it have to be so complicated? Is the woman being so difficult that the only way you can get audience is by associating yourself with her amateur theatricals? And it's so un-bloody-subtle. All that public demonstration!'

Tom felt winded. He had not imagined that his preoccupation with Jonquil could be so easily detected. All he could manage was, 'I didn't know it was obvious.'

'Obvious! It sticks out a mile! And I can't understand it, never seen you turned on by anyone like this before. I admit she's talented, but how you can take her egotism I just don't know. Honestly, Tom, you must know that all Julia is interested in is promoting herself.'

Tom gasped as the air rushed back. 'I think I'll cope,' he answered.

It was hard to disguise his relief. Dave's misinterpretation was understandable but he did not correct it. He had no longer any inclination to confide.

'Hope you don't mind my going on like that.'

Tom shook his head, smiled, then did not know how to stop.

A voice from below called that supper was on the table. Tom had been waiting for that, and though he had fled his solitary kitchen in search of guaranteed nourishment, he followed the proven form: he descended to the hall in advance of Dave, opened the front door and shouted, 'I'll be going then, Mrs Aspinall. I don't want to hold up your meal.'

'You'll not hold us up,' she answered, coming out of the kitchen. 'And you can stay if you like.'

Protesting that he had no wish to oblige the family to go on short rations, Tom stretched a foot tentatively over the front doorstep.

'There's plenty,' Mrs Aspinall insisted. (Plenty! Compared with what passed for food in his household, the Aspinall nosh was a feast of epic proportions.) 'Don't fuss yourself,' she encouraged unnecessarily. 'Only give

51

your mum a ring, there's a good lad. I wouldn't want for her to be put out.'

'She's out already, as it happens. I was going to do myself a chop. I don't mind sticking it under the grill. Then, if you just lend me a plate . . .'

'The idea! You'll have what we have, if you're staying. But I appreciate you not wanting to be a bother, Flower.'

'At least let me bequeath you the chop.' Until he got rid of it, Belinda would not bother to supply anything else. 'It's the least I can do. Really, I'd like you to have it.' He fished the chop from a pocket. It had grown limp since he had removed it from the refrigerator and through the plastic bag it could be seen marinading tiredly in its own juice. 'Please take it.'

'I don't like to.' Her hesitation was understandable.

'You must.' Tom strode across the kitchen and added his contribution to the next morning's mixed grill. 'There you are. Do nicely for somebody's breakfast, or a chop butty when you're feeling peckish.'

'You're a caution, Tom Taylor,' she laughed.

After the meal, Dave said, 'If you don't mind, Tom, I've got the odd essay to finish.'

'I suppose I could find something to do myself.'

'Baby-sitting? Collecting material?'

'What for?'

'The Goodenough assignment. Obtaining the opinion of various women on Women's Lib.'

'That's a good idea.'

'I'm full of them. Make up a questionnaire. Market research. Which model is easy running, low on costs, has good road hold, etc.'

'That's right. I could grab them on the streets, legally. I'd rather fancy myself with a clipboard.'

'You don't need a clipboard to record the view of this

one,' Dave said, his glance flicking across to his mother who, surrendered to the vertiginous delights of Radio Four, was smiling damply at a promised Archer addition to Ambridge while she ironed an immaculate shirt. 'Have you ever noticed? What women lack is a sense of proportion. With them, it's always one extreme or the other. They never seem to manage a balanced view.'

'There are certain activities where you wouldn't want them to. You can't have it all ways.'

'I'd settle for just a few of the ways, now and then,' Dave leered.

So would I, Tom said to himself, though there seemed no way suitable for Jonquil Faulkner. There were the usual fantasies, starting well, but as soon as they reached an intense bit, they collapsed. He could not keep a grip on her. No matter how hard he tried, he could not prevent her from turning away and he would find they were back in a corridor at school, she unaware of his presence and hurrying ahead; or just as he was getting along splendidly, all hands and whispers, her voice would boom at him from a grille and all he was left with was the scratch of dry fern against his palm and a couple of lethargic sheep eyeing him from the path. Gradually, bits of her would return to him: her hair, the blue of her eyes, the flutter of her dress, but more sensual pleasure eluded him. Some barrier interposed and in a strange, contradictory way he was happy to concede it; his idea of her was inconsistent with these kinds of schoolboy dreams.

On the other hand, he argued to himself as he walked home, it was not those he should be concerned about. He should be concentrating on the real thing, finding what she was like in the flesh. (Pause for heavy breathing.) It was years before he would meet her at Gritley

Thespians — weeks, anyway. He must think of something before that. There should be hundreds of plausible reasons for approaching a woman.

This reminded him of Dave's suggestion about the Goodenough assignment. He liked it, and listed the women he could question: Dave's mother, Liz, not Belinda, one of R.G.'s sisters said to have gone back to Nature, the French *assistante* . . . Jonquil Faulkner . . . Jonquil Faulkner! That was it! He'd drop in with the questionnaire and introduce himself. It was a marvellous excuse. Bespoke. Taylor made.

'You're looking very pleased with yourself. Nice to see, for a change,' Stan Driffield said. He had the appearance of having been at the back door for some time. His dog lay disconsolate on the lawn, his nose buried in damp leaves. 'I've told him to stay there. He won't come inside.'

'How's everything, Moloch?' Tom greeted. The dog swivelled its eyes, confused.

'I was just passing. Thought I might catch your mother.'

'You have to be quick to catch her.'

Stan nodded and examined the hang of the door. 'This needs adjusting. It wouldn't take a minute, with the right tools. I could nip down one evening and see to it.'

He followed Tom into the kitchen.

'There's the new sink unit,' Tom informed him.

'Oh, yes?' The man's gaze seemed stuck on a pair of Belinda's high boots lolling against a radiator.

'Down here on my right,' Tom helped the other to find his bearings. 'It's O.K., except the seal with the wall is a bit dicey.'

'Really?' Stan strode across to the sink, activated by

purpose. 'You're right. A real mackled job. This muck needs raking out and a piece of two by two, bevelled, taken the whole length. I'll bring a bit along.'

The man's eagerness for work was impressive. It was an emotional fixation. Tom wondered how you could lapse into such a state.

'When did you say your mother would be back?' Stan asked.

'I didn't. No idea.'

After that, conversation became less animated. Tom made two mugs of coffee. Stan examined the content of his, but appeared reluctant to succumb to its ambiguous temptation. Tom worked out several opening lines but speech was even more difficult than before, now that they both wanted the same woman.

However, he could not afford to let this knowledge inhibit him.

'Aren't you building the set for *A Taste of Honey*?'

'Yes, but it's not a big job. Only the one.'

'I hear Jonquil Faulkner is producing it.'

Stan looked up, surprised. 'Oh, no. Fenton Strachan's producing, but he wants Jonquil for Helen.'

'For Helen?' He could not believe it. 'But Helen's so old!'

'One foot in the grave, no doubt, from where you are standing. She's only forty or so.'

'But Jonquil would have to look *awful*, all flabby and coarse, as if she's past it, like a real old pro. Why don't they get someone nearer the right age and looking rotten? There are dozens of them about.'

'That has been said, though it wasn't put quite like that. However, they are impressed by what she has done elsewhere. She's very experienced and apparently read Helen well. Fenton wants her; he's very taken.'

Another rival! The place was crawling with them. 'He must be half blind. I mean, she's not the right type. And she's far too good-looking, and her hair is all wrong for it.'

'She can wear a wig.'

Tom leant against the table. The conversation had left him shaking.

Stan examined the skin wrinkling round the edge of his mug.

'Tom,' he said, 'there's something I'd like to say to you, but it isn't easy, and I can guess what you'll think about it, coming from me.'

His next words were mumbled, then submerged by the sound of gears and an engine revving up to take the drive. The car passed the window, braked, exploded into reverse and shot back into the garage.

'Is that your mother?'

'Dad. Belinda can't manage that manoeuvre with such panache.'

Then Mike was coming through the back door, followed by the dog. 'Hello, Stan! Long time no see. Why's this poor devil shut out?'

'I was just going.'

'That's no reason for leaving you in the cold, is it, boy? I wonder sometimes whether we should foster some hound. It could exercise Belinda. Don't hurry off, Stan. If you haven't anything pressing, you could join me in a drink.'

Stan sat down again. 'I dropped in to return a book Belinda lent me. Have a quick word.'

'She won't be long. I'm hoping for a word with her myself. I haven't seen her much this week. Been away since Tuesday.'

'I don't want to get in your way . . .'

'Good God, man, I'm not going to grab her as soon as she walks in! I do have a sense of occasion. And in any case, I'm tired.'

Stan looked miserable. 'Had a hard day?'

'Foul. I spent the afternoon closeted with an idiot. A computer salesman. He talked about storing my bytes on floppy discs and wanted me to enthuse over his user-friendly compatible systems! You having a beer, too, Tom?'

He declined, citing an unwritten essay, and as he left them he avoided Stan's eyes. He did not mean to leave Jonquil Faulkner to Stan's attentions. That was what the man had been about to suggest.

Chapter Five

Tom stood under the shower, naked except for his socks. He soaped himself thoroughly and watched the lather slide down his legs then collect above the dams of wool. He flicked his feet to encourage the foam to soak through but only succeeded in dappling the bathroom wall in a grey spittle which dragged down the tiles leaving thin tracks of scum. So he turned down the water, picked up the packet of detergent he had providently brought in, and poured a good coating over each foot. Standing on one leg, he rubbed at the sock with the sole of his free foot, kneading the wool so that the mixture was well blended and watching with satisfaction the deepening colour of the water as it oozed out. He changed to the other leg to discover if the second sock held such riches.

'From the age of seventeen,' he soliloquized as he worked, 'Thomas Taylor was in training for a lover. Before this date, a different programme had been conducted by his mother who argued that just as women learn simple household tasks, so men should serve an apprenticeship in domestic drudgery, and she held on to this belief despite the reasoning of her forbearing son. Namely, that men only become husbands when accident or reckless promises have forced them to change their state; that few heroes in literature choose this inferior status; that when a lover enters matrimony, interest in him ceases and the novel soon ends.

'No wonder then that the condition of lover is much sought after and the training undertaken with zest. His horizon is no longer bound by sink and cooker.' (Tom turned up the water for a final rinse.) 'No, the lover discovers new delights in Nature, in solitary meditations upon the moor.' (He climbed out of the shower and began to dry himself.) 'And he enjoys the mysteries of twilight and darkness as he patrols the neighbourhood of his mistress's abode.' (He studied his skin for blemishes.) 'His imagination is inspired; his brain fertile with schemes and plots.' (But the areas behind his ears resisted examination.) 'And things before undreamed of become alive with possibilities.' (However, the rest revealed no wart, blackhead, pimple, carbuncle or boil – a truly schoolgirl complexion, which was a mind-blasting cliché if ever there was one. Then he removed his socks, laid them on the floor and tramped out a heady-looking liquid.)

'And every day, by simple, artistic strokes, the lover enhances the lives of those around him,' he concluded as he hung the socks on the radiator.

In his room, he sat at his desk, found a clean piece of paper and copied out a letter already drafted.

Dear Sirs,

I have a complaint to make about the enclosed product. It is stated on the guarantee that your inner soles improve foot, sock and shoe hygiene for at least two months. These have been worn during normal working hours for four weeks only and their efficacy has ceased. It was never very good in the first place. Therefore I am accepting the invitation made on the guarantee to return these soles in the expectation that you will replace them with another pair, preferably unused.

59

Before closing I should like to take the opportunity to point out an error on the accompanying leaflet. It states that Sweeter Feet are 'specially designed for the maximum ingestion of common pedal vapours'. Vapour is not ingested, but inhaled, a fact which will have been demonstrated to you on opening this packet, and I wonder whether this expression contravenes the Trade Descriptions Act.

Yours faithfully, etc.

Tom stapled the letter to the soles and put them inside a large envelope filched from his mother's study. Then, taking a sheet of scrap paper, he headed it 'Questionnaire on Women's Liberation', and began the main business of the evening.

Question 1: When did you first become aware of the movement?

Question 2: Have you taken part in any of the following: consciousness-raising groups, conferences, fund raising, protest marches, relevant strikes?

Question 3: Have you read any of the periodicals? State which.

Tom turned over the page and discovered that he was writing on the back of Belinda's latest note. He reread it. 'Tom, these socks *stink*. They will contaminate everything else in the washer. I refuse to handle them. Either change more often, wash more often, or stop sweating.'

He slid from his chair and pranced up and down the room. 'I like it. I like it, you indefatigable woman. It's got rhythm. Question 4: Do you think men should change more often, wash more often, or stop sweating?

60

Five: Do you think men are inferior to women, superior to women, or different? Six: If a man made you a proposition would you slap his face, ask him to elaborate, or immediately accept?'

Tom lay on the floor and executed a few press-ups to work off some of this sudden energy. He was growing into a manic depressive, one moment crotch deep in misery, the next flying astride cloud nine and giggling like an idiot.

And why did he feel this now? he asked himself. Because tomorrow afternoon, Saturday, he had a date with Jonquil Faulkner. There she will be, preparing herself a frugal meal, a bit miserable at the prospect of eating it alone but glad of the respite from Tarzan who will be sluicing himself inside and out after his weekly wallow in the Rugby pitch, and suddenly her drab afternoon will be enlivened by unexpected and stimulating company. Tom's.

Of course, there were other contenders in the field: Tarzan, Stan Driffield, the producer at Gritley: he told himself to reduce the heavy breathing to manageable pants, but he had several advantages. For example, his age. Some people, either envious or self-excusing, claimed that youth had everything going for it (though he had not noticed that much himself). But, in any case, he looked older than he was, at least as tall as Tarzan and Stan, with a good stubble if he left it a couple of days and a decent chest without having to go in for constant maintenance.

He lay back, thinking about the next day.

'I can see you're impressed,' he said to Sarah, later that evening. She was sitting on the table in the living room, studying the questionnaire with silent concentration. 'I should be interested to have your opinion.'

Sarah picked up his pen. Very tentatively she touched the paper with the nib and examined the mark.

'We can skip the first three questions and the ones on your parents' marriage. What about number six, whether girls are conditioned to go for less responsible jobs?'

He ran his fingers under the words and Sarah followed with the pen, spraying ink in its wake. Then she rubbed in the drops vigorously with her free thumb.

'Fine. Now look at number seven, the use of women in advertisements.'

He pointed to it and Sarah set to work with the pen. 'You see, women claim that it degrades them, being made into sex objects, and I sympathize.' Sarah got the nib through the paper and began stirring to widen the hole. 'On the other hand, as I've said to Belinda – but she's too pigheaded to listen – women ought to admit occasionally that all this interest in them is flattering; it shows men's appreciation. Frankly, I wouldn't mind being a sex object myself.'

Sarah looked up and considered him.

'All right, don't push yourself. What about question eight, whether women should alter their appearance to attract men? Sarah, I'd rather you didn't try to tear the thing up. You've made your point. Which makes me hesitate to mention you have ink on your nightie. About time to call a halt, as they say – i.e. time for bed.'

The suggestion was boring. Sarah yawned. Then she looked at him, alert, her eyes glinting. 'Moloch,' she demanded.

'I'll do Moloch for you,' he conceded. 'Only there has to be a pact. You have to be mature about this. You come to the lavatory, clean your teeth and get into bed and I'll Moloch in the bedroom. O.K.? That's called bribery, one of the main methods of bringing up children. No doubt you are already familiar with it.'

Sarah indicated its familiarity by rising quickly and lurching upstairs.

Tom lifted her on to the lavatory seat, surprised by her lightness and the narrowness of her chest, then, feeling shy in front of her practical manner, he went into the bathroom and looked round.

As in the kitchen, a degree of improvisation had gone into its furnishings: a beer crate held nappies in tight scrolls; a pram provided lodging for toilet rolls and jars of cream; panelling, springing away from the bath, opened up territory for extra storage. Tom got on his knees and peered. Just inside were detergents and cloths for cleaning; further in, under the bulbous belly of the bath, was a shallow tray crammed with packets, envelopes, a bakelite compact. A word caught his eye.

'Christ! She's not taking chances! She must send the Family Planning Clinic bananas!'

He pushed the packets of Durex aside and opened the bakelite compact. The dome of rubber, squashed by the lid, popped up at his touch. Its size amazed him and he wondered how such a thing would be accommodated. Experimentally, he squeezed the ring round the edge of the cap until it became a blunt ellipse. Thus shaped, it looked more manageable, a truly remarkable device, he decided; aesthetically a low scorer, but for practical purposes undoubtedly a Good Buy. Tubes of spermicides, cans of foam and applicators were less interesting. He put them away and hurried on.

He had just reached the pills when he felt Sarah nuzzling against his neck. 'Moloch,' she reminded him.

'Hang on. You climbed off the seat yourself, didn't you? You should have waited for me.'

She dealt him a look which expressed her opinion of his slow service before pointing to the tray. 'Mummy's,' she rebuked.

'Yes, but she won't mind my looking. Nearly through, then we'll go and Moloch.' He selected a small wallet and removed the card. Together they scrutinized the rectangle of transparent bosses filled with plump pills. Tom counted aloud: twenty-one, with another in the centre marked, Last Tablet.

'You know, this is something I hadn't thought of,' he told Sarah, gesturing towards the tray's contraptions. 'And I need to. I mean, it would be nice if I needed to, wouldn't it? I ought to go prepared, follow the worthy Baden-Powell's precept, not like Dave with that girl in the Lakes.'

Sarah had no time for discussion. She had poked a hole in the foil behind one of the plastic bubbles and was picking methodically to extract a pill.

'Those aren't Smarties, my girl. You're not intending to put that in your mouth, are you?'

She frowned at him and shook her head.

'These remind me. I forgot to include them on the questionnaire. Apart from contributing to higher research, it would give me some useful knowledge to work on. How's this? Which method of contraception do you prefer: Dutch cap, pessary, Pill, coil, French letter, abstinence, sterilization of male?'

He grinned. She smiled back. They giggled. Then Tom was taken by uncontrollable laughter, rocking on his spine like a snotty-nosed Third Former, legs doubled up, eyes closed, belching out gusts of hysterical breaths,

mouth open. Into which, hand poised until the gaping
jaws swung under, Sarah neatly dropped the pill.

He thought about that as he left the house late the next
afternoon, amusement giving way to anxiety. For he had
swallowed; the stuff was circling around his system and
he wondered whether it was responsible for his present
queasiness. He knew there could be side-effects, but were
they usual after only one? There had been no immediate
symptoms; he had been able to mongrel about for Sarah,
make a clean copy of the questions, read a little, engage
in brisk economy-pack repartee with Liz. The pill did not
begin to affect him until he was getting ready for this visit
– shower, shave, change of clothes, hairwash, nails
clipped, Mike's deodorant lavishly applied, much
arrangement of forelocks, pen filled, the rest gathered
together. Once again he checked on the packet of Durex,
borrowed unopened from stock but now half empty after
quality trials the night before. He patted the clipboard
under his arm, looked at his watch and chose a circuitous
route through the town. Perhaps a good walk would
stabilize his pulsing stomach.

Gazing unseeingly into the main fish and chip shop
in the centre of town, he became aware that his attention
was sought by someone inside. Ellard Richardson,
decked in white apron and starched cap, was brandish-
ing a wire scoop over the shoulder of a waiting customer. Tom felt obliged to go in.

'Hang on, Tom, I want a word,' Ellard shouted, then,
'Sorry, sir, what was it you was after?'

The customer was Roland Goodenough. He acknowledged Tom in an abstracted way, opened a bag and
addressed Ellard.

'I have returned, Richardson, because it seems you
have made a mistake. My order was two fish and chips

but there are three fish here.' He scratched around and produced a rectangle, battered in the approved manner and showing signs of wear.

'That's all right, sir. It's on the firm.'

'You mean you have stood me an extra piece, Richardson?'

'Well, not exactly.' Ellard hastened to give new life to the fallacy of honour among thieves. 'I just slipped it in.'

The man's throat twitched. 'But you must not give away other people's property, Richardson! I appreciate the thought, but I cannot take it.'

He held the piece across the counter. A crack appeared along the cooling shell and a few barnacles of batter fell away, carrying with them loose entrails of limp flesh.

Ellard plucked the carcass from him, reinterred it among the chips and sealed the grease-spotted paper over it with three dextrous slaps. 'Don't you fuss, sir. I'll see it's all right.'

Mr Goodenough hesitated. 'You make it very difficult for me, Richardson. I don't like to refuse a gift, but I'm not sure that I can regard this as one.'

' 'Course it is. On the level. Why else would I done it? Anyway, the old man'll never miss it. You can see it's a second.'

'You can't help some folks, can you?' he commented when Goodenough had stumbled out.

The exchange had raised Tom's spirits. In spite of the greasy fumes, his stomach had settled and his head no longer ached. He wondered why he had delayed his visit to Jonquil for so long.

'I say, Tom, you know that girl you go about with sometimes?' Ellard asked.

'Which one?' They leered together.

'Her with the legs and knockers, not big, but up . . .
you know.' Ellard demonstrated. 'Her ass swings when
she walks. Yeller hair.'

Tom frowned. He could not recognize the description.

'Her dad's a teacher, only not at our place.'

That detail was more helpful. 'Kate Morrison?'

'That's her. You going regular?'

'Christ, no! She's just one of our lot.'

Ellard looked relieved.

'You rate her, then?'

Ellard signified her rating by some bass-clef gargling
which doubled him up and sprinkled the wilting chips.
Recovering, he explained, 'She's different from that lot
in our year. Got style. I like a bit of style.'

'I wonder what your chances are. I mean, she is older
than you,' Tom added hurriedly. The idea of Ellard
even approaching Kate was ludicrous and also, somehow, disturbing.

Ellard poked through the chips, hooked out a crisp
one and flicked it into his mouth. He gave it a few
savouring chews, rolled it into a wad and tucked it in
his cheek. Then he leant forward. 'Let me tell you
something, Grandpa. It's not your age birds is interested
in. It's your equipment.'

Tom repeated that observation to himself as he
climbed the road from the centre of town, wondering
whether Ellard's equipment ran to Durex and clipboard.

There were few people about now. Nearing the moor,
Tom could see the remaining cars of dedicated sight-
seers parked along its edge; the occupants stared out at
the darkening slopes and listened to the radio, taking
the air on trust. Above them, alien figures disturbed
their steamy vision, heavy-booted walkers who used

the moor as stomping ground to improve muscle and wind. Tom reflected that his own needed drastic restoration as he turned into her road and, panting, staggered to the gates of the house.

For a time he stood, one hand on the stone gatepost, and watched his finger trace the carved name: Camelot. The romantic illusion of a Victorian mill-owner sickened him; it was an ironic comment on his journey, yet appropriate to the emotions he felt. Which were released once more in harsh, painful breaths. At last he turned, and walked through the gates.

He kept his eyes straight ahead as he went up the drive, passed between the snarling beasts and climbed the steps. Through the stone portals, he stood in the antechamber where paling sunlight came lambent through the ruby glass. A small panel glowed by the side of the inner door. He read her name, luminous, warm, inviting.

There was no wait this time after he had pressed the button.

'Come straight up,' her voice invited, and he passed through the second door, crossed the wide hallway and strode swiftly up the curved flight of stairs, his fingers skimming the polished banisters, his eyes admiring the cornice's moulding, his ears ringing with the chimes of the words she had spoken. It was going to be all right. She had called to him from her bower, wanting him to come. An arrow pointed, the shaft gilt, the vanes glossed raven. Like her hair. Down the stuccoed corridor his steps echoed, crisp, unfaltering, and the door stood open.

He stood on the threshold. Again her voice called, and he entered in.

Flames in the open hearth leaped to greet him. A

carafe of wine stood on a silver tray. Satin cushions plumped the sofa and spilled over the carpet. Lamps touched low tables with reticent light. The scent of food cooking spiced the air.

From the next room her voice came again. 'Shan't be a minute. Help yourself to a drink. You're earlier than I expected.'

Then she was there.

She was the quicker to recover. 'I'm sorry. I assumed you were someone else. I didn't ask who it was, did I? You're . . .?'

'Thomas Taylor.' He was dizzy. He could not adjust.

'I remember. Didn't we meet once in the corridor?'

He nodded. Light, before shaded, now beamed blindingly. He put up a hand to protect his eyes.

She crossed to a lamp and switched it off. The movement was brisk, hinting impatience. Then she lit a cigarette and stood by the hearth, one arm resting along the ornate mantelpiece. In spite of his confusion, he noticed the theatrical pose. 'Nice of you to drop in. Any particular reason? Not that you have to have one, of course, but it is more usual.' Her smile was amused, slightly flirtatious.

He clutched the clipboard to him and recited the rehearsed lines. They were his introduction, his only way into the scene and he had to get through them. Their familiarity was a crutch; improvisation was impossible while his brain still spun.

'I don't mind answering a few questions.' She was not looking at him. Her eyes were going about the room, checking that everything was right. 'But I must put the finishing touches to this meal, so I'll have to call out the answers.'

She went into the kitchen and Tom sat with the

clipboard under his hand, knowing that he had missed his chance.

The next five minutes were agonizing. He would shout a question and she would yell a response. As this progressed, his voice died on him and the interview became disjointed, a sequence of laborious repetitions.

TOM: (*croaking*) Do you think girls . . . are conditioned . . . by education . . . to believe themselves less able . . . to hold positions . . . generally dominated by men?

SHE: (*loudly*) That's a long one. I didn't quite catch. Conditioned by what? Oh, I see. Yes, I suppose some are. It all depends, doesn't it?

HE: (*hoarse*) . . . the use of women in advertisements . . .

SHE: (*fortissimo*) Can't say I've paid much attention.

HE: (*piano*) . . . encouraged to alter . . . appearance . . . attract . . . men.

SHE: (*stentorian*) You'll have to speak up. I've got two gas rings on and a tap running. To attract men? Why not?

HE: (*whispering*) . . . underline your favourite novelist . . . Jane Austen . . . Norman Mailer . . . Barbara Cartland . . . Thomas Hardy . . .

SHE: (*screeching*) Will you repeat that? I'm afraid I don't read much. I took O-level literature, though, and one of the short stories was by D. H. Lawrence. Will that do? Who is Marilyn French?

Tom looked down at the paper wearily. Her answers disappointed him. He had not bothered even to mark them in. He would think about that later, if he could bear to. He suspected that it was important. He turned the clipboard over and rested his elbows on the back.

One more squeaking communication, and he would be off. He cleared his throat and breathed deeply.

But she entered, drying her hands on a towel and flicking her sleeves back to her wrists. 'That all? It was rather short.'

'Yes.' He was glad the sheet was covered.

'Short and sweet, eh? I approve of that. I'm sorry I was so little help. To tell you the truth, it's not a matter I've paid much attention to. I suppose I should, but I've never needed to, if you see what I mean.'

He did not, so he said, 'Thank you for giving the time to it, anyway.'

'No trouble.' Again her eyes went round the room, checking the prepared scene. He rose.

She stood by him at the door; fingers ringed with silver rested against the frame. She barely topped his shoulder and there were only inches between them. He tried to summon words and the inches remained.

Attempting to ease his departure, she asked, 'Do you always scribble on the back of clipboards?' For a second her hand touched his as she tapped the wood.

Focussing was difficult. 'My baby-sittee did it.'

'Your baby-sittee?'

'I baby-sit, so she's baby-sat. I'm the baby-sitter, so she's the baby-sittee,' he explained ponderously.

'I see,' she said, without conviction. 'So you go baby-sitting?'

'That's right.' He was at the door, dejected by more than failure.

'I must be losing touch. I thought you Sixth Formers spent your leisure time burning up the countryside in high-powered cars . . .'

'I haven't got a car.'

'. . . chasing the girls.' She was untroubled by his

stare. 'Or madly playing soccer. I never thought of baby-sitting. Do you enjoy it?'

'I'm addicted.'

It seemed a long way back to the front door. Outside, dried leaves on the steps crackled under his feet, rousing the crouched beasts whose spines arched in the dusk. Shadows lay deep in their mouths, lengthening the teeth. Beyond the gates, the twilight was a refuge, a necessary concealment. Then a car came down the road. Its lamps held him, exposed, until it turned into the drive he had just left.

Is it always like this? he asked himself as he stumbled away.

Chapter Six

It was no more than a mile home, most of it downhill. That was fortunate; he was in no condition to attempt more exacting gradients. The autumn dusk was thickening, curdled by a mist which gusted in patches like smoke from garden fires. Although this was appropriate, it was altogether too thin and tentative. Tom would have preferred to be marooned in an uncompromising, impenetrable fog.

The presence of a figure in the porch and the obligation to acknowledge it was an intrusion. Probably Stan, looking for a job. Unwelcoming, Tom greeted him.

'Hi,' Dave answered. 'Thought it was you.'

'I live here.'

'Your mother was wondering where you were. She's dashing about, making a meal.'

'She's inclined to when Mike's at home. He brings out the worst in her. Do I gather that you've already been inside?'

'I called to discuss some scripts she's been reading.'

'Already? You don't waste time, do you? Any joy?'

'Joy? Oh, I see.' Dave blushed. 'We've had a long chat. She has been very helpful. Has quite a lot to say about them.'

'I bet.'

'That was the reason I asked her to read them, wasn't it? You made the suggestion. I should never have bothered her otherwise. I think it's very good of her to give time to them. I must seem miserably small fry to her.'

'There's no need to get so heated,' Tom answered, surprised. 'Isn't the present novel going so well?'

'The present novel?'

Tom reflected that conversation with his mother had left Dave strangely confused. He nodded, sympathizing.

'Oh, the one I've been on recently? I've thrown that out. I've got another idea.'

'Any good?'

'Different. Not so much plot, more . . . feelings.'

It was unusual for Dave to be evasive. 'If you'd rather not tell me . . .'

'It's difficult to explain. And you might not approve.' Then, as if to prevent further questions, he added, 'Incidentally, there's a happening at R.G.'s tonight. Very select. While his parents are away.'

'Shall you go?'

'No, I want to work on this idea. But Julia's going. R.G. thought you would like to know that.'

As it happened, that was the last thing he was interested in at that moment.

Tom stood in the bathroom and examined his face. It did not look any different from when he had set out. That was strange. Disappointing. You would have expected a line here and there, a hollowness round the eyes, a suggestion of silver at the temples as evidence of what he had been through. He had balled up the whole thing. Pathetic. After that set-up!

The trouble was, she was not interested and he had not had the sense to leave it, try something else. What? He supposed he could have managed some light chat, shown an interest in what she was cooking. She had been anxious to put the finishing touches to her dinner.

Why did she have to express it like that? It did not do her justice.

Her answers to the questions were funny, when you considered them; not in themselves but in their effect upon him. He had expected a different response. He had not anticipated her indifference. As far as she was concerned, the subject did not exist. Which did not mean you put her in the same category as Dave's mother.

He could not understand why this should matter. He really had got himself into a mess. She was intelligent, otherwise she would not be in her job, and talented, for apparently she could act. Nor was that the sum of her attractions. His breath laboured as he thought of them.

It would have been marvellous if the meal really had been intended for him. He imagined the firelight, cushions, the carafe emptying while they talked. They agreed that the lamps were unnecessary, that they could relax more comfortably on the rug where the warmth encouraged them to shed superfluous garments . . .

He had begun to fumble. She moved to accommodate his hands.

But he could go no further.

Tom filled the hand-basin and scrubbed at his nails. So much for that. A few more sessions of that kind, and he would be so loused up he would never be able to go near her, let alone anything else. Absently he began to shave and had finished before he recalled that he had done so already that day. Then he could think of no other occupation. An essay on the treatment of courtly love in the *Franklin's Tale* failed to attract. Neither did a party suit his mood. But going to R.G.'s might provide a distraction.

Also it seemed a pity to waste the shave.

*

'Pleased you've come,' R.G. welcomed. 'Drinks in the kitchen. Help yourself any time. Alka-Seltzer alongside. The master bedroom, with integral bathroom, i.e. my parents' little cell, is out of bounds. Otherwise, spread yourself as you think fit.'

'I'm not thinking fit at the moment.'

'Then you need some of this to tone you up. A special brew.' R.G. ladled about half a pint of punch into a tankard. 'I must go and put another record on. Must keep them on their feet as long as possible.'

Tom followed, looking into each room as he passed. R.G. was a good host and spared no trouble in preparation. There were fires in every hearth, dim lights, bowls of nuts and crisps, cushions scattered to replace some of the lighter furniture, stacked somewhere unseen. He had rolled back the large rugs in the sitting room, so big that its boundaries were not touched by the light from the open fire, and was now in the centre of the dance, partnering two girls simultaneously with much ingenuity and vocal accompaniment. Tom responded to his signal and began some idiosyncratic gyrations at the edge of the floor.

'Shall I take your glass?' Betty offered. 'You can't dance properly while you're still holding it.'

'I intend to dance improperly.'

Betty, never particularly bright even at her best, took some time to puzzle that out. 'I see. You're late. It's been going ages. I always arrive right at the beginning.'

Tom wondered whether another mouthful of the punch would brighten up her conversation. He sipped experimentally.

'That's because my father won't let me be out after one o'clock, even for a party. He comes and collects. In the middle of the midnight movie.'

76

'My father doesn't generally watch it, so he hasn't the same incentive to turn out.'

'Oh, Tom, I'm so sorry! You've mentioned that before, I mean, how you manage. Don't think I'm interfering, but if you ever want any help, you've only to ask.'

'Have a refill.' R.G. interposed a bottle. 'Punch is off now, but this stuff is better. À la carte.'

Not halted by the interruption, Betty continued, 'You will ask, won't you? Don't think I'd be putting myself out.'

He reflected that, despite her protests, she was putting a good deal of herself out at that moment. It loomed up at him out of the twilight. He drank some of the wine, at the same time anchoring himself firmly to her waist. 'Thanks. I'll remember that, Betty.'

She smiled at him gratefully. 'You know, it is only when you are standing like this that I realize how tall you are.'

'Perhaps we ought to sit down.'

'I daren't, else I'd never get up.'

He had a vision of her, forever stranded upon a heap of cushions, while R.G.'s father strode round her, finalizing business deals with well-tailored guests. 'I didn't know I was so irresistible,' he said.

'Oh, it's not that! I've promised to help R.G. serve out the supper. You know what he's like. Has to have everything just so.' She removed herself from his grasp with sighs which he took to be regretful and disappeared into the dusk.

Tom considered following her, but finding the going difficult, stopped at a convenient sofa and flopped down.

'You like some more?' a voice asked. 'Why not? Here, hold your glass.'

A bottle glinted at his elbow, borne by an arm whose lack of covering continued to more parts, further off.

'I like your dress,' he said, though harness would be a more appropriate word, he decided.

'I always wear it at parties. It's my mum's. We're the same size.'

'Lucky you. I can't enjoy the same benefit. I'm quite a lot taller than my mother.'

'Fellers often are, aren't they?'

Tom thought it was time for another dose of wine. The result was encouraging. 'Haven't I seen you somewhere before?'

'Don't know. I work in Mr Grimshaw's office.'

Tom modified his concept of R.G.'s father. Manufacturing worsted appeared not to stifle more exotic tastes. 'Sounds like a nice office. I must drop in some time.'

'Why not? Reg does, when he can get off.' She perched on the arm of the sofa.

'I can appreciate why.' After a considerable amount of wrenching and poking he contrived to get an arm behind her and latched a thumb through a guy at the front. She wobbled slightly but kept the bottle under control by wedging it upright between her thighs. Tom tried not to look at the structure.

'Wouldn't you be more comfortable down here?'

'Why not?' Ideally shaped for the manoeuvre, she rotated ninety degrees and slipped backwards on to his lap. The bottle remained clamped in position.

'That's clever. Is it one of your party tricks?' he asked, trying to suggest that the time was now ripe for its removal.

She ignored the question and with an expert flick of her arms lassoed his neck. His head came down and there was a clink of teeth upon glass. Not wishing to mar the occasion with petty complaints, he attempted to adapt his embrace to the obstacle but after a few trial runs discovered that the only solution was to clasp it also. Four minutes later, the threat of third-degree bruising caused him to desist.

'We could get rid of this if we emptied it,' he suggested.

'Why not?'

This expression was beginning to lose some of its original charm but, still game, he stretched for their glasses. She extracted the bottle and poured.

'There's some left,' she announced, rattling it against his ear.

That finished it. Tom took a deep gulp and sat back. 'Perhaps you ought to nip round with it, then.'

'Right.' She levered herself from his knee. 'Won't be long.'

The promised return was not desirable. Tom decided it was expedient to be on his way.

This was more hazardous than was expected. The route was littered with discarded shoes, none of which came in pairs – a fact which caused him to ponder upon the possible anatomical deficiencies of the guests; and there were a good many feet protruding from odd gaps, again arranged in apparently random permutations of size, shape and choice of hose. Tom groped along, pausing at various stations of rest until a chink in the blackout revealed legs which struck him as familiar. The only trouble was that the feet at the end of them were aligned the wrong way.

'Why are your big toes on the outside?' he asked.

'Probably because I've got my legs crossed,' Kate answered.

She was sitting with her back against the wall, her skirt ruched tight across her thighs.

'I like your dress.' He had an idea that he had mentioned that before, so added, 'As I've already said.'

'You haven't.'

He could understand why she had not heard the first time. The volume on the record player had been raised another fifty decibels for the few dedicated contortionists who remained in the middle of the floor. So he shuffled closer, put an arm behind her neck and repeated in her ear, 'I like your dress. And it's a good party, isn't it? When you can find anyone.'

'Find anyone? You've been falling all over them! Or have you mislaid one or two?'

Tom giggled. 'I like that, Kate. I really do.'

'I thought it was rather good myself.'

'I didn't exactly mislay them, Kate; they walked off, perhaps because I had missed laying them. The question is, does there have to be a lay before it can be judged to be a miss-lay? Or put it another way, when is a miss-lay not a lay?'

Kate sighed. 'I'll just feed you the lines and you can ruin them.'

'I was only trying to clarify the concept for you,' he explained. But the effort had tired him. His brain, he decided, must be temporarily out of condition, and other parts of him were behaving in sympathy because his breathing was difficult, too. He attempted to improve matters by resting his head against Kate's.

'Oh, why don't you piss off?' she retorted.

Tom did not wish to do that. Sitting next to Kate was surprisingly comfortable, in spite of the trouble he was having with his breathing. Generally that was occasioned by something else, so he could think of no cause for it now, unless it was her hair. The smell intrigued him; it was not overpowering but a faint, elusive scent he could not put a name to. Each time he sniffed he was certain that he would distinguish it but he never did, so had to sniff again.

'Have you got a cold as well?' she asked.

'As well as what?'

'As well as your other disabilities.'

'I wasn't aware that I had any.'

'People rarely are.'

'No one else this evening has noticed them,' he answered, sulking.

'They wouldn't. They appeared to have other things on their minds.'

Clearly Kate's defective hearing was compensated by superior vision, since squinting across the room he could see no objects clearly behind the curtain of shadows.

'They weren't very exciting,' he admitted.

She gave a coarse snort.

He realized that his comment was equivalent to an apology. This irritated him. He had no idea why he should suddenly explain away his behaviour to Kate. Childishly, he demanded, 'Anyway, what's it to do with you?'

'Nothing,' she snapped.

Angry with each other, they did not speak. But neither did they stir. Tom's arm remained behind her neck in spite of the cramp spreading to his shoulder and she made no sign that she wished it removed.

'Would you like to dance?' he asked eventually.

'I'm resting. There was quite a heavy start to the evening.'

With whom? he asked himself. 'In that case, I'll take

a turn solo. Just a number of private, meditative convolutions.' It appeared that lucidity was edging back.

She laughed. 'I should wait till you can stand straight.'

'That is not necessary.' He gestured to the centre of the room where the staggering remnants still persevered.

She laughed again, a series of gruff, generous notes.

Surprised, Tom found their effects upon him pleasurable. He grinned at her, considering.

'Why do you have to be such a clown?' she asked him.

'You'll have to rephrase that. I can't answer it as it stands.'

But any further demand for logic seemed inappropriate. He had never thought of himself as a clown. While he was doing so, R.G. joined them.

'Supper's up. In the kitchen,' he announced. 'Sorry to intrude such an ordinary business into intellectual discussion.' His glance took in the rest of his guests whose occupation could not be so described.

'Nothing intellectual about this discussion,' Kate said, rising.

'Hard to believe that when you're here,' he answered, putting an arm round her.

'Honestly, R.G., you have the most peculiar ideas about me.'

'Not peculiar. Very straightforward, as it happens.' Gripping her shoulders tightly, he kissed her quickly on the cheek. 'Only I know my limitations.'

'You surprise me.' She grinned, flirtatious. 'Why not try to overcome them?'

'Any more encouragement like this, and I might take you up! Trouble is, the flesh is willing but the brain is too weak.'

'And what's brain to do with it?'

'Not a lot, but it comes in handy. Also, it's necessary with someone like you. Did you know, Tom, she's doing a splendid job on my O-level language? Aren't you, Teach? After her tuition, I might even pass!'

But Kate's face had gone sombre. 'Don't evade the issue, R.G. What was it you were implying – about brain being necessary with someone like me? Do you mean that because I'm bright I put fellers off?'

'There, you are! That proves it. Straight on the nail, isn't she, Tom? Don't you worry about it, my dear. That's their fault. I'm only talking about dim fellers like me. It's our loss, not yours. You're my favourite girl, only I decided ages ago I'd be wasting my time.'

Kate stared at him. 'Oh, R.G! What a thing to assume!' Her face screwed with the effort not to cry.

'Now then! You're a lovely lass, but a bit daft, seemingly.' He leant to her, put his hands to her face, then suddenly drew back. Abruptly he was again the host. 'What a bloody way to go on! At a party! Let's forget it, shall we? Supper's waiting. Tell you what, you two stay here, and I'll send something in. No need to fight your way through the mob.'

He strode away, and it was some time before either of them spoke.

Tom was astonished. He had not guessed that R.G. held any amorous feelings for Kate, or indeed that she could inspire them. He wondered how long she had.

He felt sorry for R.G. He knew what it was like, though R.G.'s inhibitions over Kate were different from his own with Jonquil. Or were they so different? he pondered. Different because it was not intelligence that created a barrier but similar because there was a barrier he could not overcome. And it was of his own making.

This afternoon she had said, 'Nice of you to drop in. Any particular reason? Not that you have to have one, but it is more usual.' Surely a hint had been there, and he had not picked it up. How could he have been so dense? But the hint had been there. Things were not so hopeless as he had thought. Perhaps next time . . .

From somewhere, he heard a voice whisper. 'Tom, do you think I'm like that?'

'Like what?' he asked absently.

Kate stared at him, disbelieving. Then her face puck-. ered.

Understanding broke in. Beginning to shape words of apology and consolation, he stretched towards her. But touch was prevented.

'O.K., you two. Break it up. Look what the fairy godmother has on offer tonight.' Julia dumped a tray on the floor and arranged herself artistically beside it. 'Clean glasses and a bottle of plonk, to be followed forthwith by dishes of oriental preparation borne by lackey in glittering livery.' As she gestured, a figure appeared behind her. 'My God! He's straight on cue.'

It was Ellard Richardson. He was wearing a heavy donkey jacket, large areas of which were reinforced with brilliant orange plastic. Along each arm were balanced two plates of curry and rice.

'What a waiter, Ellard!' Tom complimented.

'More like a forklift truck, slightly animated,' Julia corrected.

They each took a plate and Julia handed out forks, omitting Ellard, but he extracted one from a pocket and began to eat.

'You're staying?' Julia asked. From which it could be deduced that Ellard's standard attractions had failed their guarantee.

'Might as well,' he answered blandly.

'Help yourself to a cushion, then,' Kate invited.

'Well, wasn't this a nice idea of R.G.'s?' Julia smiled at Tom, brilliantly. 'Away from the hurly-burly, he said. I've been trying to get to you all evening, but I got tied up. Very boring.'

'Tom's been the same,' Kate told her.

'Let me pour everybody a drink,' he offered. It was at such moments that he could understand why some people take to the bottle.

Kneeling, Julia held up her glass, its bowl cupped between both hands. 'Nectar!' she declared in ringing tones.

Tom looked despairingly at Kate but she turned her head and addressed Ellard. 'I'm impressed by the donkey jacket.'

'I got it this afternoon. Special.'

'Sounds interesting.'

Watching her being interested, Tom emptied a liberal helping of wine down his throat and did not object when Julia arranged herself round him.

'You heard them fire engines, late on this afternoon?' Ellard leant to Kate, his face intent. 'It was a warehouse, up by Gill Moss, and our Doug came into the chippy, soon as word got round and he says, pack that in now, Ell, you're coming with me on the bike, and I says straight, knowing that something were up, you look after the counter, Alf (that's the fryer), while I take a quick break, and Doug says we'll see's you're all right, Alf, with a wink, and so up I was on the bike and Doug goes like the clappers to Tetlow's warehouse, worried, you see, he wouldn't get there before it had all gone. But it was all right; there was plenty. The firemen had finished and the fuzz looked the other way while us and a few other fellers went over the stock. Some of it was in a right mess, ruined with the water. Them firemen don't care. Never stop to think. Just see a wisp of smoke and they'll put the hose full on it, the mean sods. Anyway, we didn't do so bad, piled a lot on oursens, you know, starting with the smallest sizes and then going up. We looked a right pair of nurds when we'd finished. Then we roped some more together and fastened them round us shoulders and we were off. Would you like a donkey jacket, Kate? I'll give you one. On the house.'

'The warehouse, perhaps.'

He chuckled. 'I didn't know you was funny as well.'

'As well as what?'

The following exchange was lost to Tom since Julia, irritated that his attention to her had been rather perfunctory during Ellard's narrative, now claimed his ear, deafeningly close, and began a sensational report on Gritley theatre, her forthcoming part and how she intended to play it. Protection seemed necessary. Tom emptied his first glass and got a good way with a second. By this experiment he appeared to hit the right dosage because thoughts were impinging less harshly and with every sip his environment was growing more comfortable. The latter was also helped by Julia's assiduous ministrations.

Eventually it came up no surprise to discover that his head was resting on her lap, from which position he heard Kate say, 'No, Ellard, I want your honest opinion. Do you think I'm an intellectual snob?' and Ellard's enthusiastic response, 'Of course you are. Else you wouldn't be in the Sixth, would you?'

An uneasiness scratched through Tom's languor. Some intervention was required of him but thought was slow, half-formed and elusive. Yet an indistinct memory caused him to mumble, 'Kate, that wasn't what R.G. meant,' but all he received in answer was a fierce stare and a toss of the head.

He tried to raise himself but his chest was hooped by locked arms and fingers were gripped over his brows. It was odd how he could be clamped down yet suffer from vertigo. Peering along the floor, he could not get his bearings in the twilight for the terrain was unstable and features swayed or slid away, only allowing themselves to be captured if he screwed up his eyes and stared hard. He pinned down a cushion, let it bounce aside, caught a couple of empty plates, released them and watched them crawl crab-like across his vision.

Meanwhile his ears were tickled by whispers. These gradually grew pleasurable, full of promise: Fenton thinks she's good . . . playing Helen . . . rehearsal . . . Jonquil Faulkner . . . meet . . . next Friday.

'Not soon enough,' he stated loudly, feeling suddenly bold.

Laughter followed, tinkling against his ear. His objection had been accepted. Arrangements were being made to meet earlier. He heard directions, concluding with, 'Don't be long.'

His support sank, floated away from him, and he lay washed up on cushions. She had said he was not to be long. He began to lever himself up. This took some time, and when he had his torso almost vertical he rested. His new position brought him close to an unusual detail in the decor he had not noticed before. This was a luminous orange patch, suspended about a foot above his head. It was part of a P.A. system because it crackled and began to make an announcement. Concerned with the problem of finding firm ground for his feet, Tom paid no attention until it addressed him personally.

'Sorry to have to ask you, Tom, but can you just lend me the one? Or maybe a couple? You never know.'

Tom puzzled over the request as a hand came out and assisted him.

'Never go anywhere without, but I dumped my anorak this afternoon,' Ellard explained. 'Forgot to take them out of the pocket.'

Higher up, the air was clearer. It circulated a few sluggish currents of comprehension. 'Any time, Ellard.'

'I'll give you them back.'

'Don't bother. I don't fancy them secondhand.'

Ellard giggled. 'You know what I mean.'

'In any case, these are free samples. Hang on, I can't find the pocket.' It was lucky he had gone baby-sitting the previous night. If it had not been for Liz, he would not have them. If it had not been for his mother, he would not know Liz. He paused, thinking that over, before continuing his search. Finally, he admitted, 'I haven't any. There are no pockets in this damned sweatshirt. I must have left them in my jacket.' The one he had been wearing that afternoon.

'Both in the same shit, then. Still, thanks for the thought. I'll manage. And you.'

'Thanks.' Tremors were shaking the room again; the effort of concentrating with Ellard had brought on a relapse.

More or less upright, Tom began to grope along the wall. There must be a door somewhere, but they had moved it, which was not fair; it threw you out. They altered the routine as soon as you got used to it: announcement on the P.A. system, then straight through the door and up to the flat. There were also people he had not noticed before; they kept crowding in his way. There was noise, too. A record player that had been mumbling shyly to itself suddenly erupted close to him, its blast throwing him across a heap of other victims. Sadly, misfortune made them irritable: 'Watch it, you nurd!' and 'Get moving. You're standing on my leg.' Extricating himself, he crawled away.

It was quieter in the hall but the glare of lamps after the twilight outside was so dazzling it was necessary to close his eyes and feel along the corridor. This resulted in his missing the staircase, but there were plenty of rooms to choose from and squinting through half-closed lids he decided to check on these first. By the way they had been changing things round, it would not surprise him if she had moved to the ground floor. He grappled with a handle and, hearing a voice, pushed.

Tom stood on the threshold. Again her voice called, and he entered in.

Flames in the open hearth leaped to greet him. A carafe of wine stood on a silver tray. Satin cushions plumped the sofa and spilled over the carpet. Lamps touched low tables with reticent light. The scent of food cooking spiced the air.

She was sitting on the rug in front of the fire, her back towards him, and the light fabric of her skirt was fanned over the floor in gauzy folds. Against the light her hair was black, a shadow with unfathomable depths which streamed over her hand as, reaching back, she sifted the dense mass at the nape of her neck. Then she turned.

'Close the door, Tom,' Julia said.

Chapter Seven

'We'll draw a veil over the rest, if you'll excuse the expression.'

'Granted. But come on – you can't chicken out now! When I've built up a scene I don't omit the climax,' Dave argued.

Tom reflected that he had already omitted a good deal. The description of the party had started well: a quick moving, racy account with plenty of sexual innuendoes, witty comment and satiric observations, but as it progressed the number of admissible details was reduced and he had to resort to dramatic pauses to think his way out. Now he could not tell Dave what he had expected as he opened the door.

'It was an anticlimax, really.' Dave could not know how true that statement was.

'Didn't quite get to the point, then?'

'As a matter of fact, I fell asleep. More precisely, I passed out.'

Dave hooted. 'I like it; I like it. You spend weeks wandering around looking desolate and the first time the girl shows willing, you pass out! It's rich. How did she take it?'

'I can't say. She'd gone when I woke up.'

'Now is your chance to find out,' Dave said as Julia, with Pin and Kate, crossed the common room towards them.

Tom braced himself. It was essential to retain Julia's

goodwill. Now that she had committed herself to the part of Jo, she did not need his encouragement. But she was his ticket to the first rehearsal. If he did not attend, Jonquil would be no more accessible in the future than she was now.

'The lover's brain becomes fertile with schemes and plots,' Tom recited to himself as he greeted her heartily. 'And things before undreamed of become alive with possibilities,' as he threw out his arms and hugged her to him.

'Wow,' she said, delighted.

'You're looking great, Julia.'

'Flatterer!' she exclaimed, clearly agreeing with his judgement.

It occurred to Tom that perhaps the only thing actors responded to was acting. Behave normally, and they grow suspicious. Testing the theory, he bent over her and muttered incoherently, 'Julia, I don't know what to say about Saturday night. I feel such a . . .'

'What?' she demanded.

He gave a furtive glance at the others, careful not to catch Kate's eye. 'You know,' he whispered. 'I feel awful about it, I really do, dropping off like that.'

'Perhaps it was as well,' she enunciated loudly. 'You were pissed rotten.'

Tom hastily revised his theory. 'Anyway, I'm looking forward to the first rehearsal.'

'Aren't we all? And I'll make damn sure you don't pass out at that!'

So the previous arrangement had not been altered; he was expected to accompany her. Tom smiled at her affectionately, incautious with relief.

'R.G. says he will take us in his dad's car. He'll pick you up about twenty to seven, Friday.'

Friday! Five days to get through. Tom did not know how he would manage. One way to fill in the time was to study the play, but that idea had to be postponed since Julia, prattling about Gritley Thespians, steered him out of the common room and towards Roland Goodenough's lesson. It seemed diplomatic not to object.

As it happened, he did not regret that he had attended. Mr Goodenough had a problem he was anxious to share.

'As you are aware,' he began, 'we adopt in these dialogues a loosely structured approach allowing for full and frank interchange of opinion in an atmosphere of trust which we are, hopefully, building towards a flexible reciprocal understanding to create a forum for those issues of conduct . . .' – the loose structure of his lessons having infected his style, Mr Goodenough groped to complete his sentence – '. . . and such an issue I myself would like to introduce today which, in my experience, I have to admit, is unique.'

He was wearing a leather-buttoned cardigan, shapelessly knitted by his spouse. Two pockets were concealed at the seams. Goodenough pushed his hands into these, linked them under the generous folds, and looked at the faces of the Arts Sixth. Momentarily, he reflected upon the incapacity for surprise that afflicted today's youth.

'What I have to say concerns a young man, a member of this school – naturally I cannot name names but I can rely on you all not to let it go further than this room when I say that he suffers from a degree of emotional deprivation, since his mother works as a barmaid and is unable to supervise her family in the evenings, which you will recognize as a clear case of female-role dissonance. This young man compensates by seeking the affection of others, to which end he has procured a donkey jacket of the kind worn by road-menders and has asked me to accept it as a personal gift.'

'Oh, isn't that sweet of him?' Betty exclaimed moistly.

'I'm afraid it is not as simple as that, Betty,' Goodenough answered, avuncular. He liked this girl. She had – and he made no excuse for the old-fashioned word – soul, quite different from some of the others who were having difficulty in hiding their amusement. 'You see, he has not purchased the jacket. Indeed he has told me frankly how he comes to have it in his possession.' Goodenough narrated the circumstances of Ellard's acquisition. 'The point is, not to mince matters, I regard that jacket as stolen.'

He paused. There appeared to be a distinct atmosphere of levity in the class.

'He claims that the police "looked the other way", that the owners had "slipped the fuzz a fiver" to help get the stock off their hands, so making the way easier for them over insurance!' Mr Goodenough continued unhappily. 'It is terrible that a young boy can hypothesize that such corruption exists! And if I accept the jacket the very person who should set him an example is as much as telling him he can continue such conduct.'

'Why not tell him to get lost? I can't see the problem,' Pin said.

Roland Goodenough flinched. Not for the first time he regretted having agreed to include an engineer among the Arts Sixth. This boy Pin had a disturbingly simplistic approach to ethical problems. 'Can't you see that if I did that I should reject his appeal for a caring relationship which might disorientate him, emotionally, for life? Think of that.'

They thought of it. By that time most of them had

picked up that Ellard was the boy Goodenough might disorientate emotionally. It seemed improbable.

Goodenough looked round desperately. 'I am asking your opinion as to what I should do. You have the terrible alternatives: a connivance with criminal behaviour or rejection.' For a moment, emotion improved his style.

'There may be a compromise,' Dave began slowly.

'That's right,' R.G. came in. 'What about this? It would put you in the clear if you said you would have the jacket – only insist you pay for it.'

'*Pay* for it?' Goodenough echoed, outraged. Attempting a gesture of dismissal, he dragged a hand from under the folds of his cardigan. It emerged, mittened by a clinging pocket.

Tom said, 'But your premise that the jacket is stolen may be wrong. If so, you can accept it.'

'I cannot regard it as anything other than stolen,' Goodenough replied dismally.

'You have to look at it from his angle if you are trying to find a basis for contact,' Dave argued. '*He* believes that he has done nothing wrong. You might do something immensely destructive to that young boy's psychology if you were to suggest that what he had done *in all innocence* was a criminal act.'

Goodenough paled but a fugitive intellect prompted him to say, 'That comes close to condoning the total denial of personal responsibility.'

'No, you are adopting a too legalistic position,' Tom told him. He leant forward, lowering his voice as he had done to Julia; practice might refine the effect. 'It's a matter of trust and needs extremely delicate handling. That boy trusts you, of all people, to believe that he is acting *in good faith.*'

94

Goodenough nodded. 'I hadn't thought of it like that, Taylor.'

There followed an analysis of the discussion, in which Goodenough brought to their notice the occurrence of certain seminal phenomena such as the spontaneous role assumption in the group and the dynamics of the interaction which had facilitated decision-making and the development of mature conceptual insights in a way which had been for them, as it was for himself, such a meaningful learning experience.

After the lesson Tom succeeded in evading Julia and hurried to the library. It was essential to begin work on *A Taste of Honey* without further delay because it had occurred to him that Jonquil, so terribly miscast as Helen, would need a lot of assistance. Finding a suitable occasion to give her that would require some ingenious planning but he would deal with that problem later. Reaching the library, he found Kate already settled in.

'You might like to know that Nanny Childe is issuing warrants for your apprehension,' she told him, without looking up from her book. 'He wants to see you, plus UCCA form suitably completed.'

Tom decided that one day he would have to allow Mr Childe to catch him but, at present, applying for university entrance was still low on his list of priorities. He said, 'You know, Kate, I could do with you as a secretary.'

'That's the last thing you'll have me as.'

'Thanks for volunteering. But I might be more interested in the previous things.'

'Don't flatter yourself. They're not on offer.'

'Surely the "last thing" assumes that others have preceded it? Look at the sentence rationally.'

'Sorry, I prefer to listen to the emphasis. Sometimes, Tom Taylor, you are an unmitigated bore.'

Holding the book, her hand was arched, small and delicate. On the middle finger her pen had raised a small cushion of flesh.

'Only sometimes?' he asked.

'I don't know about occasions when I'm not present.'

'Thanks. I appreciate your scruples.'

She looked up at him quickly, then away. 'You provoked that. You always do.'

'I know. Why is it?' Genuinely puzzled, he stooped over her and the scent of her hair came up to him. It was associated with a jumble of memories from the party: her laughter as she called him a clown; his inadequate response when she had appealed to him, followed by her distress. He wanted to apologize to her but could find no immediate way of doing so. 'Why do you get at me so much, Kate?' he asked again.

'That's a big question,' she answered him. 'How long have you got?'

'All day, if necessary.'

'I thought you might say that. Unfortunately I haven't. I haven't opted out of the conventional routine, so I was thinking of planning an essay.'

'Thinking doesn't commit you to it. What about a cup of coffee first?'

'In order to indulge your vanity? Not likely!' But she was smiling now. 'It'll save.'

'It might lose its spontaneity if you brood on it too long. Why don't we meet in The Crags this evening? There's a new barman there. He might overlook a couple of underage pints.' Kate's company was suddenly more attractive than studying a play.

'I can't. I must get this essay written for Nanny Childe.'

'Another night, then. Not tomorrow; I'm babysitting. Wednesday O.K.?'

'I'd like to, Tom, but I've got so much work on this week. Friday would be the best time.'

'Fine,' he answered quickly. Then he remembered. 'Oh, Christ! That's no good, either!'

'What full diaries we have!' She laughed, then stopped abruptly. Her lips pursed. 'Of course. How could I forget? Incidentally, have Gritley Thespians been notified that Julia Marshall will be bringing her manager?' Lowering her head, she sniffed and bent over her book.

'So I slunk off,' Tom explained to Sarah the following evening. 'It's hard, lounging about, when there's a girl strenuously ignoring your presence. And the strange thing was, I would have liked to tell her about it, though I can't think why I wanted to get it straight.

'On reflection, I'm pleased I didn't,' he continued, wiping away the jam that Sarah had smeared along his sleeve. 'To convince her that I wasn't interested in Julia would have required me to explain about Jonquil, and Kate would be even more disapproving of her.'

He munched through a remnant of sandwich which Sarah stuffed into his mouth. She had the habit of chewing round food, kneading it to the consistency of paste and thrusting the artefact upon him. Tom now regretted having conceded these evening snacks.

'If you eat any more of that, my girl, you'll soon be too heavy to sit on my knee.'

Undismayed by the prospect, Sarah stretched for another sandwich.

'All right, just one more. Then you're for bed.'

'Mung. Story,' she answered.

'Later. Don't be selfish. Don't you realize I'm in a mess? I hope it's worth it, Sarah. I hope all this subterfuge is successful. It might be. After all, love will find a way, an overworked cliché of mind-blowing optimism. It wasn't said with Jonquil Faulkner in mind. And the rest of them are growing more than I can cope with. When I go into the common room there's Julia ready to emote all over me; if I drop into a lesson there's Kate looking daggers and cutting me dead, if you'll excuse the mixed metaphors.'

Sarah indicated her forbearance by stroking his cheek with a finger encrusted with jam.

'To conclude, I'm sorry to say this, Sarah, about your sex, but women are a strange lot and I'm thinking of putting in a formal complaint to one of them. Correction. Not one of the common mould. She belongs to a subspecies: my mother. Obsessed with training me as a mate, she concentrates on cleaning, mending, washing, looking after babies, when she should be providing intensive tuition on the fundamental problem. Women.'

'Story,' Sarah said, as soon as he had finished.

'Right. Upstairs and the usual routine first.'

That completed, and the sheets arranged to her liking, Tom sat on the bed and began. 'Once upon a time there was a young man. Every day he would walk to school and skive from lessons and eat his dinner which was mainly mashed potatoes and custard. In the evening he would walk to Sarah's house and give her orange juice and Moloch for her and tell her stories.'

Sarah nodded, approving.

'Then one day he fell in love with a beautiful young woman. Her name was Jonquil.'

'No!' Sarah interrupted. She scrambled up and pushed at him, trying to move him off the bed. 'No! Not Jon!' and burst into tears.

It took him some time to soothe her and she was not fully appeased until he had got down on the floor and performed the Moloch shuffle accompanied by the verse.

'You are a funny girl, suddenly crying for no reason,' he rebuked, as he pulled the sheets round her again. 'Only silly women behave like that. Last time it was Julia. I wouldn't want you to grow up like her, Jammy Face.'

Sarah smiled, wriggled, and drew her arms from under the bedclothes. She laced her fingers together, looped them round his neck, and pulled. This time he understood what she meant.

'Could you manage again this week?' Liz asked, three hours later.

'Baby-sitting?'

'Got any other ideas?'

'Not at the moment.'

'Pity.'

'Yes.'

'Fine. Friday, then.'

'Sorry, Liz. I've got something else on.'

'Damn. I'll have to ask her next door. She's forever stuck to her Hoover. Anything interesting happening on Friday?'

'I'm not sure. I hope so.'

'Still playing hard to get, is she? Or is there competition? You want to beat the rush and catch the bird.' She perched on the arm of his chair.

'I think there are others interested.'

'Don't you be put off by that.'

'I'm not.'

'Women don't like fellers that dither. Rather they got in and grabbed.'

There was more of Liz under her voluminous dress than seemed possible. Tom concentrated on the hypothesis that it could affect her balance. 'I don't think that she's that sort.'

She leaned over him. Tom observed that her dress was cut lower than he had hitherto noticed. 'What you pinch them for, then? Own up. Look me straight between the eyes.'

Her face was so close, Tom had no alternative. 'Pinch what?'

'You've been under the bath. Why's that, if you don't think she wants?'

'I hope you don't mind my borrowing a packet,' he enunciated carefully.

'Help yourself. Only don't flatter yourself it's you I'm thinking about. Don't you think that.'

'I wouldn't make that mistake.'

'There's a button nearly off your shirt,' she observed.

'Betty can't have sewn it on very well. Do you feel like having a go?' Routine might provide a distraction.

'No, that's your job. A stitch of thine saves mine. Betty's her name, then?'

'No. Betty is just a girl in the Sixth.'

'Just a girl in the Sixth!' Liz swung round to face him fully. This action brought her nearer leg over the arm of the chair and into forceful contact with his. 'Choosy, aren't you?'

'Depends. You should see Betty.'

'That's no reason to get at her.'

'It's no reason to get with her, either.'

'So she's not in the Sixth, the other one?'

Tom was wondering whether it would help matters if he were to ease his leg away. Knowing it would, he desisted. 'No, she's not.'

In addition to the leg problem he was now experiencing the usual trouble with his breath. Tom found this perplexing. 'I think it's time I went,' he managed.

Without rising, Liz stretched across him and picked up *A Taste of Honey*. 'You been reading this? Funny, that. It's at Gritley in November. That's why I'm out Friday.'

Tom looked down at her as, half lying across him, she flicked over the pages. Pulled by her movement, the neck of her dress revealed skin still brown after the summer, faint at the nape but deepening along the spine. 'I don't follow,' he answered her, trying to work out an excuse for investigating the extent of the tan.

'I'll be at the theatre.'

'So shall I.'

'You working backstage?'

'No; looking in at the first rehearsal.' It was disappointing that she had sat up.

'So that's why you can't baby-sit!' She regarded him. Her thought was as elliptical as her language. 'I see.'

He blushed. 'I didn't know you were interested in the theatre,' trying to deflect her interest.

'Stan roped me in.' She was impatient with explanations. Then, 'They say she's good.'

Evasion was impossible. Liz already knew he was not pursuing a girl in the Sixth, so Julia was discounted. 'I hope so. What worries me is I don't think she is right for the part.'

'How?'

'She's not like Helen. The whole thing is out of character.'

'She's supposed to *act*.'

'How can she possibly do a coarse, flabby old pro? And she's far too young.'

Liz drew breath to speak, paused, looked at him, reconsidered, and said, 'She'll cope.'

That was what Stan had said to him. It was strange that he was not offended by the prospect of Jonquil's playing Helen. Clearly you could not anticipate how people would react, even a rival. Tom heaved himself out of the chair.

'I didn't know you knew Stan,' he said, reflecting that, despite his infatuation, the man did not limit his attention to Jonquil. He still had time to offer a joinery service to Belinda or to build sets in the provocative company of Liz.

'It's a small world.'

He felt depressed. His pursuit suddenly seemed hopeless.

'Incidentally, I'd be grateful if it didn't get round about Jonquil.'

'What you take me for?' she demanded, following him into the hall.

'Sorry.' He looked down at her. Her hair was neither long nor coal black. Instead it was reddish brown, the tight curls brushed into an uneven frizz which had netted small whiskers of fluff. He bent down, thinking to pull them out.

'Time you were off,' she said briskly, as if calling him to the task ahead. 'And don't fret. Remember, love will find a lay.'

Chapter Eight

During the remainder of the week Tom decided to devote his time to *A Taste of Honey*.

'I wonder if I could work in the English stockroom during free periods?' he asked Mr Hardy.

'I'm not sure that it is suitable for permanent residence. Do you not regard most of your lesson periods as free?'

'I only skip the odd one. I don't understand how I have this reputation.'

'Then your skill at interpretation is less developed than I thought. However, if you are indicating a desire for solitude in which you may engage in a little unexacting work, may I suggest that you employ yourself in exploring those English texts to which a degree of study still remains to be devoted? In your case, Taylor, a very great deal. Also, may I remind you that it is customary to clarify your response to them and to set down thoughts, should any be forthcoming, through the medium of short dissertations or, as they are named here, essays. Apparently this is not a literary form which you find congenial, Taylor, since few examples of your attempts to master it have come to my notice this term.'

'I've written the essay on the madness in *Hamlet* but I haven't quite completed the conclusion. I'll let you have it as soon as it is done.'

'How very cooperative of you, Taylor! Whilst

commending the scholarship which requires you to spend three times the prescribed time upon it, may I warn you that certain compromises have to be accepted, however distasteful. You are entering for A-level, not a doctorate. Therefore, conclude that essay briskly and deliver it before lunch. I shall expect the remaining three essays set this term to be handed in by the end of the week and shall be interested to see in what way the dust and dereliction of the stockroom has inspired their composition.'

Following Mr Hardy's advice to be brisk, Tom sketched a few ideas round the quotations he had noted the previous evening and filled six pages. Though short on content, the essay was strong on style, which he considered an achievement in the limited time he could allow.

Then, at last, he took up *A Taste of Honey*.

He had not seen the play in performance. His knowledge of it rested upon a quick reading a year or so earlier. Though he remembered it quite well he had forgotten Helen's gritty capacity to survive and her physical attraction. Even so, he remained convinced that Jonquil was unsuitable to play such a woman: domineering, cruel, selfish, brash, loose, going to seed. Liz had said that she would cope; to do so, she would certainly need a lot of help.

For a start, she would have to apply plenty of wrinkles and generous padding round the hips to suggest a middle-age spread; and if she were to wear too tight, skinny blouses, she would probably give the illusion of an overblown tart, even if the shape did not sag. Her hair was the worst problem but Stan had mentioned a wig. A horrible peroxide blonde would be the best.

Technique was another matter. Tom rose from the

table and read a few lines. After experiments he thought he had found the right way to deliver them, but the style demanded movement so he removed piles of books from the floor, arranged a couple of chairs, decided on entrances, demonstrated moves and gestures, and began to direct Jonquil in the cleared space.

They got on fine, not paying much attention to Jo /Julia's lines, and when Peter entered, Tom switched to his part. Adopting a swagger he considered appropriate for a car salesman, he quickly got the feel of it, brought in Helen /Jonquil, and they went over the pages together. The result was invigorating; he had not guessed he had such a talent, and he particularly enjoyed Peter's dislike of Julia /Jo, making it clear that he wanted her out of the way while he concentrated on Jonquil. After a time, feeling in need of a rest, Tom moved to a chair and took the next pages stretched out, relaxed.

Perched on the narrow arm, Jonquil had difficulty in keeping her balance so she brought one leg over and leant against him as she read her lines. Her dress was cut lower than he had hitherto noticed and her head was close to his as she bent over the pages, so that he breathed in the scent of her hair, strangely elusive, that he could not name. She leant across him and, seeing the skin at her nape was still brown after summer, he pushed down the collar of her dress to discover the extent of her tan.

Then she was on her feet again and he pursuing her, weaving between chair and table, over heaps of books and round the rocking stacks until, discarding the text, he pinned her against a bank of shelves. For a time he experimented with more detailed aspects of production, such as the fastening of her blouse and the position of his hands, until he bent over her and, sweaty, lascivious, he recited Peter's line: 'Come on down to the church and I'll make an honest woman of you.'

It was at that moment that Mr Hardy entered the room.

Late afternoon on the following Friday, Tom stared at his face in the bathroom mirror and scraped a finger across the stubble. It was amazing how it sprouted more quickly the more frequently it was hacked down. Perhaps he ought to grow a beard. You could do a lot with a beard. One day, provided that Jonquil liked it, he would definitely cultivate one. However, it was probably significant that both Tarzan Turnbull and Stan were clean shaven. He squirted some of Mike's shaving foam over his face and set to work.

The recollection of his competitors (not to mention the producer at Gritley) intensified the pains in his stomach. He had been feeling distinctly sickly all day, just as he had felt after swallowing that Pill, but since he had not taken one recently he had to admit that he was suffering from nerves. Stage-fright. Meeting the woman you wanted was no different from going on stage and it affected you in the same way. The thought started the heavy breathing again. In an effort to calm himself, Tom cleared his throat, thereby spraying the mirror with gouts of foam, and recited from the blurb on the dust jacket of his autobiography, *Embryo and After*: 'This is a frank exposé of a mother's cynical perversions which force her innocent son into bondage, with explicit passages describing initiation rites at the kitchen sink, and the hero's courageous struggles towards a personal solution through the pursuit of a nubile, raven-haired schoolmistress whose theatrical ambitions he spares no pains to assist.'

Instead of decreasing, the panting was growing worse. Desperately, Tom continued, 'This marks the turning point in this luminous, unique, violent yet ultimately compassionate book, when, acquainted with the play and ready to advise his mistress on interpretation, the author discovers that the role of lover is similar to that of actor-manager. He has learnt a part, set the stage, manoeuvred himself into a favourable position, chosen his leading lady . . .'

'I could hear you talking to yourself a mile off,' Belinda told him as he entered the kitchen.

'Why travel a mile when you can listen in the comfort of your home? I'm feeling somewhat peckish. Any chance of food?'

'When did I not provide food?' she demanded, but continued before he could quote precise dates. 'There's a casserole in the oven. Leave enough for Mike, but none for me. I'll have something at the end of the evening. You can get quite a decent meal in a wine bar.'

'Thanks for the tip. A pity I've no chance to make use of it. I didn't know you were going out. It doesn't say so on the calendar.'

'I don't put all my engagements on it.'

'Are you saying those up there are only the published ones? Is there a subtext I have to deduce?'

She laughed. 'I hadn't realized that you studied it so closely. I'm going into Leeds, a meeting of the Writers' Circle.'

'I thought you'd stopped going to that. You used to say it was a waste of time.'

'Yes; but I think that Dave will enjoy meeting a few

people in the trade, whatever the goods they are producing.'

'You're taking Dave?'

'Is there any reason why I shouldn't? Wasn't it you who suggested he should ask my advice?'

'I never imagined it would result in jaunts into town and slurping up the vino in wine bars.'

'I fancy there is a good deal that you didn't imagine when you made the suggestion,' she answered tartly. 'But if you would like to come with us, you are very welcome.'

'I already have something on.'

'I thought you might have. Talking of things on, I understand that you are showing a sudden interest in amateur drama.'

'Who told you that? Honestly, you can't do a thing in this town without everybody's knowing! Gossip is the local disease, and everyone admits it. Stan Driffield once told me that when he first came here a fellow buttonholed him in the Prize Tup. He said to Stan, "So you come from Lancashire, do you? Pity about that. Still, it can't be helped. Now. But if you take my advice you'll keep your head down and play a dead bat when the Roses is on." Then – and this is why I bring this up – he added, "And I've another word of advice that might come in handy. If you've any indiscretions to perpetuate, it's wiser to per-pet-uate them t'other side of the Pennines, and out of sight of the bloody pigeons, at that." '

'I wonder why Stan should remember that?' Belinda said. Then, hurriedly, as if to prevent discussion, 'And are you thinking of taking the man's advice?'

'I'm going to Gritley, Belinda. That's still several miles this side. I'm off with a crowd from school to

108

watch a rehearsal at the Thespians. Don't tell me that current gossip has omitted that!'

'Don't be so paranoid, Tom! However, perhaps I should mention that Julia's mother thinks Julia is coming round here this evening. Apparently there is work you must do together.'

This news alarmed him. He had forgotten Julia's parents. 'Why did her mother get in touch?'

'She didn't. I met her quite by chance in a shop.'

So that is all right for the moment, Tom thought; Julia's parents have been successfully conned.

This was confirmed later during the journey to the theatre, when Julia gave an account of her father's interrogation, her own responses and some implausible claims about Tom's concern with her academic progress; and the only drawback to the alibi he had provided was Julia's renewed gratitude that prompted her to abandon the front seat of the Grimshaw Mercedes and join Tom in the back. However, in spite of this distraction, he contrived during free moments to concentrate thought on procedure for the coming rehearsal.

They would arrive at the theatre and would follow Julia backstage to the women's dressing room. Jonquil would be there and he would say something like, 'We must stop meeting like this,' which would indicate that he was harbouring no hard feelings about his visit to the flat and help to put her at her ease since she would be a little tense before the first reading. She might want to discuss her interpretation of the part, in which case he had a few notes with him, but it would probably be best not to refer to them openly because that might put her off. Despite her scientific training she did not seem very interested in systematic research but relied on instinctive judgements, as the questionnaire had shown. Of course, that might pay off eventually, in situations quite unconnected with Gritley Thespians. Rather than being masters of reason, women were the slaves of their instincts, and once he had roused the appropriate one, his troubles would be over.

Chapter Nine

The parking space beside the theatre was crammed with cars, most of them suffering from chronic neglect, but one or two shining from the ministrations of a company mechanic. A pickup truck supporting an exhausted bicycle had been left across one corner, as if finishing off a set required to suggest a wide social spectrum. Action was provided by a sturdy woman in an anorak meticulously defacing the billboard with a piece of slate.

'I'll have a job to get in here,' R.G. said. 'Is there a show on?'

'No. It's always like this. They're a busy lot. They only have the evenings and weekends to get things done,' Julia explained.

'Time must drag after midnight,' Tom said.

Under the suspicious eye of the woman in the anorak, R.G. demonstrated his skill at the wheel with some flamboyant manoeuvring. This completed, Julia rushed away. Tom watched her run up the steps and into the main door. He felt a tingling panic. Julia was his excuse for being there and he had not anticipated separation until she had conducted him safely to Jonquil.

'Haven't you checked those once?' he demanded irritably as R.G. tried the car locks.

'Can't take any chances. If anything happens to this, I've got to be well in the clear. Asked my dad if he'd see his way to giving me one last year, when I was eighteen, but he said the vote was enough to be going on with.'

'We've got to find Julia,' Tom urged, as they entered the theatre.

'You must be joking!' R.G. exclaimed. 'She said they were a busy lot. I wouldn't like to see them pushed.'

The scene in front of them was a textbook illustration of manic labour. No doubt Stan Driffield-inspired, Tom thought. A woman standing on a pair of stepladders was dipping her brush into a tin of paint and jabbing vigorously at a crumbling cornice; a man flanked by light fittings was laying tripwires across the corridor with lengths of flex; and stretched like a chorus line up the staircase that led to the auditorium, the theatre's resident weightlifters wheezed under their loads. Apart from the refrigerator hauler, who had made the mistake of supporting his burden on his back, they were tackling the descent cheerfully, accepting mishaps with good humour and resource. Slats dripping out of louvred panels were seen as a challenge to future carpenters; it was judged that a castor knocked off a sofa would never let you down again after a touch of gum. The only discordant note was struck by the refrigerator man when the anorak-clad woman, triumphantly entering with the shreds of poster, informed him that she did not want the appliance downstairs.

'We're already booked up the final Friday and Saturday.' She turned her glare upon Tom.

'I'm pleased to hear that,' he managed.

'So what night do you want? Box office is closed now, but I'll make an exception, since you're here.'

He wondered what it felt like not to be made an exception. 'I don't wish to buy tickets. We've come to the rehearsal.'

'Well, you want to make your mind up soon, else we shall be booked up. How do you mean, the rehearsal? I thought Fenton Strachan had got a young darkie in. It won't look the same, having somebody blacked up.'

'I'm not in the play.'

'The stage staff are meeting behind the stage, but I can tell you one thing: if you're going to be any help, you'd better not be dressed like that.'

In the lavatory, Tom asked, 'Do you think if I blacked up I'd look like a West Indian?'

'At least she didn't assume you were playing the gay boy,' R.G. pointed out.

They examined the décor and admired the artistic economy which could establish atmosphere by a single box of coloured tissues and a poster for *Boys in the Band*.

'Do you think she will have gone yet? This place is a pleasant retreat but it hasn't enough to offer for a full evening,' Tom said.

'There's a bar just down the corridor.'

'I want to get into the rehearsal.'

But as they passed the door of the bar, a voice called them in. 'That you, lads? Glad to have you. What's it to be? Washing glasses or cleaning the pumps?'

'Neither at the moment, I'm afraid,' Tom said.

'Like that, is it? Aren't you the lads Maud's sent? She said to tell you she'd checked, and Stan Driffield doesn't need any more for labouring tonight, so you can help set up the bar.'

'We're going to the rehearsal.'

'Yes, she said one of you seemed to think you are playing the coloured boy, but she's had a word with Fenton and, like she thought, he's got a young chap up from college. Left Fenton doing his nut. I mean, the

Gritley Thespians aren't like some, and Fenton more so. If he needed a one-eyed dwarf with a hump, he'd find the real thing.'

Tom wondered what had caused Fenton to abandon this principle when he had cast Jonquil. 'But I never wanted the part!'

'That does you credit. It's best to accept your limitations. Well, I'll have to get on.'

'I'll give you a hand,' R.G. offered.

'Thank you. That's Christian. The name's Jack.'

'Reg,' beginning to take off his jacket.

Preferring not to witness further personal disclosures, Tom left them and returned to the small area inside the front door. There, activity had not ceased but was entering the second act. Still balanced on stepladders, the woman was experimenting with a new technique of rubbing down the surface before applying the paint; the electrician had discovered a cavity under the floorboards and was trying it for fit; the sofa had shed the rest of its castors and three men were performing an autopsy upon it with an electric drill. Maud was not at her post. Tom looked round cautiously, saw her through a door driving a sewing machine and, squeezing past the prostrate refrigerator hauler, rushed up the staircase. At the top was a door marked 'Auditorium'. Panting, but not allowing time for indecision, he pushed it open.

Inside, everything went black. Also warm and airless. Panic-stricken, thinking himself afflicted with instant blindness and on the point of suffocation, Tom struggled for breath. The effort brought little oxygen but a strong scent of toilet water, lavishly applied.

'I'm pleased you've come,' a voice said. 'I'd rather not go in alone, late, because, from what I can hear, our Fenton's in a bad mood. You know what he's like.'

114

'No, I don't know what he's like.' It seemed that the darkness could be some natural phenomenon. Tom felt round, exploring the terrain.

'Hey, stop that, else I'll turn you in!' the other reprimanded. 'Are you new here? Don't know the great Fenton Strachan? He's a good producer, can manage some bewitching effects at times, but mean with it, when he's a bit off colour. That's why I didn't feel like barging in.'

It was then that Tom realized that they were standing in a narrow gap between the door and a curtain hung to block out any slit of light. He stepped away from the side of the door and examined his companion in the sliver of light that edged through the crack. He could make out little, except that there was no beard.

'Are you playing Peter?' he demanded.

'That would be the day! With Nick Ainsworth around? I'm taking Geoffrey, the gay one. Not that I'm keen. You can imagine what people will say.'

'They don't confuse characters on stage with the actors.'

'Christ! Where have you been hibernating? Of course they do, and half the time they aren't wrong, either. I mean, you have to relate to the part, don't you? You have to find a bit of it in yourself, at least to start with. Are you playing the black boy?'

This was more than Tom could take. 'No. Do I look as if I could?' he snapped.

'I haven't brought my glasses. Mind you, I don't have anything against colour, myself. It's like everything else. We have to learn to live together, don't we?'

At that point a voice, originating a good way off but projected with such accuracy that it pierced the curtain and sliced between them, demanded, 'Would it be too much to ask if those people could stop their twittering? I'm trying to block in a play, and I can't hear myself think for a bloody tumult going on behind a drape. Either find some other place for it, or come right inside.'

'Knickers!' the other groaned. 'Here goes,' and pushed through the curtain.

'Well, if it isn't our Trev! And he's brought a friend!'

All eyes switched to Tom. He had the feeling that, having made such a sensational entrance, he was expected to utter a brief speech, but he contented himself with a crisp nod, walked down the aisle and selected a seat. Further along the row was a tousled woman with a script, nervously picking her nose with a pencil, and a neat-featured young man of West Indian extraction whose quiet snores indicated that he was taking a rest from his drama-school exercises in relaxation. Tom turned his attention to the stage.

He knew immediately what point they had reached in the play and Fenton must have skipped some pages because they were already in the scene after Peter's second appearance; Peter /Nick Ainsworth and Julia were sitting on a settee and there appeared to be some confusion over the exact location of a box of chocolates and a bunch of flowers.

'Helen leaves them on the sideboard,' the woman near Tom reported, scrabbling through her script and deciphering her record of the moves.

'Thank-you-Doris,' Fenton said. 'Do you mind? Now, you two, I don't like to disagree with Doris because she is supposed to write down what I say, but, according to my moves, the flowers are on the table. Julia, you take them over on the line . . .'

Tom wondered whether he might have done better if he had adopted Peter's method of bribery. Perhaps

116

women did fall for flowers and chocolates. He could not imagine them working on Belinda but they might have been worth trying on Jonquil. If you could carry off the cliché of a bunch of flowers and chocolates poking from under your arm, it might look rather dashing and romantic. When he stood in her room, anticipating her face as she saw them, knowing that any moment she would appear from the kitchen, calling her greetings . . .

'Jo, where's my hat?'

The voice came from the wings. It was shrill, impatient, Lancashire and coarse. In the next minutes, while Fenton was dealing out moves, Tom made an effort to adjust to the sound. More was needed for Jonquil's appearance.

She was wearing a short skirt made of cheap fabric with a satin finish. It was very tight and the reflection of the lamps on the shiny surface highlighted her belly and hips so that her natural slimness was transformed to a condition that, however hard he tried to find more acceptable synonyms, Tom could only describe as fat. It was a truly remarkable piece of deception and his sole criticism was that it was rather overdone. Clearly he would have to speak to her about it.

'We'll fill in the precise details later,' he heard Fenton saying.

'Can you give me some idea now?' Nick /Peter asked. 'You know how it is, Fenton; you can't learn the part without the moves. I have to know how you want me to do this.'

'What he's saying is that he wants to imagine himself at it,' Jonquil said, and they all laughed.

The line referred to was Peter's 'Got your blue garters on?'

When reading the play, Tom had given considerable thought to the production of this question and had worked out several alternatives. He had experimented with the simple gesture of stroking his hand along the thigh but keeping it outside the skirt; he had gone on to lifting the skirt and searching for the garter underneath; and, finally, he had got down on the rug and ducted an investigation that was more thorough and unimpeded.

However, none of these possibilities was being explored on the present stage, a fact which Tom deplored until he saw Nick casually tap Jonquil's buttock as he said, 'O.K., Fenton, that feels fine.'

Tom found the movement disturbing. He also disliked the way the hand, competent, well shaped, fuzzed with black down, continued to pluck the cloth over Jonquil's thigh. Keeping a supervisory eye on it, Tom saw the hand suddenly rise, flick off Jonquil's hat and carry it to Nick's head.

In the amusement and plotting of moves that followed, Tom stared upon what Nick's action had revealed. Jonquil had gone bald. No black tresses cascaded out of the crown of the hat; no dark fringe veiled the brows; no shining collar mantled the shoulders. All he could detect was a shadow capping her scalp which spread over her ears until it reached the nape of her neck. There it halted, forming a hard, black line across the flesh.

After that the play went into decline. Tom tried to maintain an interest by listening to Fenton's direction and checking it against his own notes, but he could not distract himself from the feeling of sickness, of disappointment and a sense of loss. The rehearsal was no longer important. It was tedious, a drag, yet he did not wish it to finish. The longer it continued, the longer the delay before he met her and was forced to nearer view of Jonquil's cropped head.

Meanwhile, Fenton did try to liven him up by doing a short improvised scene.

'Are you the bloke that's been talking to Maud?' he asked.

'I wouldn't claim that it amounted to a conversation.'

'You don't get parts here by barging in and intimidating Maud.'

'I can believe that.'

'And if you think I'd descend to having a white boy blacked up to play a West Indian, you're mistaken. I chased up Neville months ago.'

'You've got it wrong. I just came with Julia.'

'Keeping an eye on her? You'll have your work cut out; she can't keep her hands off Neville. Not that I'm worried. But I don't have people cluttering up the auditorium during rehearsals. You can try the pub down the road. That's where the chaperons usually wait.'

'Thanks.'

'Any good?' R.G. asked when Tom returned to the bar.

'Jonquil Faulkner has had her hair cut.'

'What was it like before?'

'Long.'

'Women are always changing their hairstyles. Now, ladies and gentlemen, what can I get you?' he inquired as the cast entered.

'Are you playing the barman?' Julia asked.

'Isn't he marvellous?'

'Type-cast.'

'And without a script.'

'I never go by the book. Leave it all to Nature,' R.G.
said, winking.

Pushed to the end of the counter, Tom recorded their
dialogue, editing the more banal lines.

NICK: Are you new to the district?

JONQUIL: Yes. I'm teaching at King James's Comprehensive.

NICK: Where Stan Driffield is. Did he put you on to us?
(*From her brief nod it is impossible to detect
whether she is aware of Stan's infatuation. Ed.
Thomas Taylor.*)

JULIA: I think I shall bring a tunic.

JONQUIL: Well, I do think it's a good idea to have the
right clothes as early as you can. It helps you get into
the part.

JULIA: Wherever did you get the skirt from?

JONQUIL: It's my own. We actually wore that kind of
thing once.

FENTON: When the rest of us were in rompers.

NICK: Our Fenton suffers from eternal youth, or so he
would have us believe.

TREVOR: (*To Tom*) How do you fit in here?

TOM: It's not the how, but whether, that's troubling me.

TREVOR: Sorry, I didn't quite catch.

TOM: Oh, for God's sake, skip it.

TREVOR: There's no need to be like that.

NICK: I don't know why you had to go and change out
of it. She's a regular tease, this new member of ours,
isn't she? Drapes herself in all this fabric so a man
can't find her best points.

JONQUIL: You're not doing so badly. But don't you think
we should wait for somewhere more private?

FENTON: Kinky!

TOM: I think that dress is very attractive. I like the full skirt; it's feminine.

JONQUIL: It's useful. Covers the bulges. Fancy seeing you here!

TOM: We must stop meeting like this.

FENTON: Like what, dearie? Are you both in drag?

JONQUIL: Thomas is at King James's. Arts Sixth, isn't it?

JULIA: (*To Neville*) Are you sure it won't be any trouble to bring me?

NEVILLE: Of course not. The only thing is, the car's not reliable.

JULIA: I adore old bangers.

NEVILLE: A lot better for you than a bus, anyway, and I could always give you a ring if I couldn't get it to start.

JULIA: That's marvellous. Did you say you could give me a lift home? R.G., do you mind if I dash? Neville can drop me off.

R.G.: O.K. by me. What about Tom?

JULIA: He hasn't finished his drink.

TREVOR: And he wouldn't accept a lift from Neville. He's not fond.

JULIA: Whatever gave him that idea, Tom?

TOM: Himself. He's just stirring it up.

TREVOR: Goes in for insulting folk, doesn't he?

JULIA: I'll leave you two to it. 'Bye, everyone. We're off.

JONQUIL: (*To R.G.*) Haven't I seen you at school?

TOM: He's trying to give up the habit.

JONQUIL: Another one in the Arts Sixth?

R.G.: You know how it is. Nobody else will have me.

FENTON: Time I was off. Mustn't miss my beauty sleep. Thanks for tonight, darling. You're going to be marvellous.

NICK: She's marvellous already. Sweet dreams, love.

(*For the benefit of readers not turned on by theatrical sentiment, the next thirty lines have been cut from this edition, but taken at a spanking pace they demonstrate the mind-blasting clichés of actors' farewells. Ed. Thomas Taylor.*)

R.G.: Will you have another drink? On me?

JONQUIL: Why not? Thank you. Should I know your name?

R.G.: Reg Grimshaw.

JONQUIL: Reg . . . Reginald . . . Grimshaw. That rings a bell.

R.G.: It's built into all our mill chimneys. My great granddad's form of graffiti.

JONQUIL: (*laughing*) No, it's not that. There's a different context.

TOM (*interrupting quickly*) I've been waiting to ask you all evening why you've had your hair cut.

JONQUIL: For the play. I couldn't wear it long for Helen. In any case, I was beginning to feel a bit of a frump with it the other length.

R.G.: I can't remember it as it was before, I'm afraid.

TOM: I can.

R.G.: But it suits you like this. Sort of curves to your head.

JONQUIL: I shall have it set up in the right style for Helen.

R.G.: Sort of frizzed at the ends?

JONQUIL: More tight than that, with waves at the top.

(*In this version, the final half-page of dialogue is covered with interpolations but the laws governing obscenity require them to be expurgated. However, from internal evidence it can be confidently stated that the scribe broke off in disgust. Ed. Thomas Taylor.*)

Tom took a large mouthful of wine and wished it would have the same effect as the wine at R.G.'s party. Looking at that meagre residue on Jonquil's scalp, he thought he could do with a patch of oblivion of the 'cease-upon-the-midnight-with-no-pain' variety. Compared with the previous heavy mass, the present style looked like a thin, abbreviated coating left after a sudden moult. Contemplation of it depressed him but, trying to persuade himself that in spite of discouragements he was still in play, he aimed a few bleak smiles in Jonquil's direction. The occasional one found its target and was acknowledged absently.

At last he said, 'I was surprised that you are playing Helen. It hardly seems you.'

She shrugged. 'It's a part, and a good one. That's all I'm concerned with.'

He had the distinct feeling that she was not interested in discussion, but Trevor's comments had worried him. 'Is it true that when you start on a character, you have to find a bit of yourself in it?'

'Now that's a sneaky one, considering who I'm playing.' She was momentarily the schoolmistress, rebuking impudence. 'I just play it as it comes. I don't go in for a lot of analysis.'

'That's Tom's hobby,' R.G. explained without malice. 'Look, Jack said he'd be back at half past to close the bar. How are you getting home? If you'd like a lift . . .'

'That would be nice.' She smiled at him.

So did Tom. R.G. must have picked up the signs. He was a good friend, quick to fall in with your needs. Pushing aside a bar stool, Tom moved into position.

'After you, then,' R.G. said, holding the door open. 'The family hearse is outside.'

'I know I'm tired, but I didn't think I looked as bad as that.'

'I should have said the family ambulance.'

Reeling from these examples of trenchant humour, Tom followed them along the corridor. Activity among the workforce had not ceased but was running down, no doubt in preparation for the night shift. The entrails of the sofa were being swept into a plastic dustbin liner; the cornice painter was inspecting the remains of the moulding; and the weightlifters could be heard advising the refrigerator man on the choice of a surgical truss. Maud was not in sight, but a surrendering scream from the sewing machine indicated that victory was assured.

There was, therefore, the setting for a smooth exit and the opportunity for Tom to introduce some mesmerizing topic which would entice Jonquil into the back seat of the car, but to his surprise R.G.'s hand was on her arm and the narrowness of the doorway prevented Tom from taking up a similar position on the other side.

By the time she reached the car, she would have forgotten his existence. He had to find some way of jogging her memory; or, if that was too much to ask, some method of attracting her notice, preferably favourable. A stage prop might help.

Frantically he looked round. There must be something lurking in the mess. Then he remembered as he saw a bowl of flowers wilting behind Maud's imperious notice: BOOK HERE.

A trial of strength followed. For the fan of flowers, carefully graded in tiers according to stage of decay, concealed a skeleton of thorny twigs and further protection was afforded by a mesh of wire at its base.

Stifling whinnies of pain, Tom latched his hands over the complete structure and tugged. It came away like a cork out of a bottle. The bowl shot across the counter through a jet of filthy water, hit the wall and exploded in a spray of fragments which glittered momentarily in a vivid flash of light as, recoiling, Tom lurched against a pile of lamps. Then darkness.

Through which, holding his damp and lacerating burden to his chest, Tom stumbled towards the door; and before the rumbling retribution of Gritley Thespians could catch up with him, he sped away.

Chapter Ten

R.G. and Jonquil had already reached the car when he overtook them. Trying to make up for lost time, Tom grabbed the handle of a door in the hope of assisting her into the back seat but was prevented by R.G.'s gallantry which owed much to the fact that he had the keys. However, he appeared to have no flowers handy, an oversight he might later regret. Cheered by the observation, Tom settled down in the back to dismantle Maud's floral device.

It was a frustrating process. The easiest part was locating the thorns but, after that, brute force was necessary to unravel the flowers from the knot of wire at the base. Those that surrendered emerged with stripped stalks and a threadbare appearance about the head which a quick shake did not improve. Instead, it deposited small patches of green slime upon Tom's lap.

Meanwhile, denied the excitements of demolition, the other two had to make do with chat.

'This is a marvellously comfortable car. Has it got power steering?'

'Yes. And it's automatic, of course.'

'That makes driving simpler, but it has its disadvantages; you can't hold it in high gear on ice or compacted snow.'

Her comments grew more technical, but he must not allow prejudice to creep in, Tom argued to himself as he plucked the porcupine.

'I could do with a car, living here,' Jonquil said.

'Would you be interested in one secondhand, condition guaranteed?'

She laughed. 'Is selling cars another of your accomplishments?'

Tom wondered what accomplishments R.G. had demonstrated so far. Meanwhile, the spiked carcass seemed to be harbouring something nasty inside.

'I don't go in for it, usually, but my dad trades in his managers' cars every forty thousand miles. If he sold you one at the price he'd get from the garage he wouldn't lose anything and you'd get a good car without a mark-up.'

'That sounds marvellous. I'd like to look into it.'

As the conversation degenerated into discussion of models and price, Tom finally got his fingers over what lay in the intestines of the wire: a flattened egg of an unripe green, pitted with holes, its surface crumbling.

'Have you any idea what this is?' he asked Jonquil.

She flinched. 'Good heavens! It's dripping all over me!' Then, as R.G. switched on the interior light, 'It's Oasis. Used in flower arrangements.'

'However did you guess that?' Tom demanded, admiring.

'It's not a guess. I went to flower arranging classes, once.'

Tom sank back.

'Dear Thomas,' Marjorie Proops wrote. 'Lots of people find this when they start going out together, and you put it very well. But don't you realize how lucky you are? She sounds a nice young girl, so why not snap out of it and join in? You may not like flower arranging, but surely you can get interested in cars? Most normal young men are. Why not attend car maintenance

127

classes? They run them at most F.E. Centres. Then you could look after her new model. Get under there, boy, in the oil and filth and start enjoying yourself! Yes, flowers and chocolates rarely fail, but I'd go easy on the beard until you've asked her opinion.'

'How do you feel about beards?' he asked her.

'Ticklish.'

Tom joined in the resultant hysteria, but it was a strain.

They were nearing home. Tom collected the flowers together and knotted his handkerchief round the stalks. When R.G. stopped at her flat, he would get out with her, follow her up the path, hand them over, and from then on play it by ear.

'I've got it!' he heard Jonquil exclaim. 'I knew your name rang a bell! Reginald Grimshaw! You're the person one of the secretaries said was asking for my address!'

There was a brief pause in which Tom began to invent frantic explanations and R.G. went in for some elaborate readjustment of the interior mirror.

'She said something about you wanting to deliver some books,' Jonquil continued. 'Of course there weren't any.'

'Well, no. I don't think there were,' R.G. answered carefully.

'So why did you want my address? I'm intrigued.'

'Oh, general interest,' he answered. By this time recovered, he turned to her, smiling.

'I don't know that I approve of young men inquiring where I live.' But in the light which R.G. had forgotten to switch off, her expression bore little doubt. 'It could be called cheek.'

'I'd rather call it initiative, Jonquil.'

128

She laughed again. Then they were stopping outside Tom's house.

'Looks as if your place has closed down, Tom,' R.G. said.

'Belinda's out.' With Dave. Close encounters of an intellectual kind in some sleazy wine bar. Lucky him.

R.G. swung round and addressed Tom over the back of the seat. 'Sorry about Julia, Tom, but she insisted on going home with that Neville.'

'Don't worry.' He wished he could indicate that the sympathy was misplaced.

'It'll just be one of her whims. All the same, I think it was a bit much. I mean, to put it at the very lowest, if you hadn't provided the alibi she wouldn't have got there. I wouldn't have done that. Have you met her father? I wouldn't go out of my way to, if I were you.'

Carried away by the thought of Julia's father, but constrained by Jonquil's presence, R.G. mouthed a vivid description.

Tom nodded. He was concentrating upon the problem of how he could remain in the car. R.G.'s silent monologue continued. Clearly Julia's father had made a big impact. R.G. began to look desperate, adding covert gestures in Jonquil's direction. Eventually Tom understood that he was asking if Tom knew where she lived.

For a moment Tom debated whether to keep silent and let R.G. find his own solution. With any luck he might not succeed. But R.G. did not know that Tom was obsessed with her; R.G. did not know that the evening's programme had been devised round Jonquil, not Julia. He was simply out to make the best of this inexplicable good fortune.

So Tom said, 'Top side. Costalot,' giving the local name.

'You're a friend.'

'You can say that again,' Tom answered as he got out of the car.

R.G. reversed into the drive, revved up the engine and hooted a farewell as he set off. Jonquil waved. Tom waved back, discovered the flowers still in his hand, shouted, and began a frantic race after the car.

There cannot be many athletes who train for the four hundred metres by running after a Mercedes with automatic gears and power steering kept in tip-top condition by the firm's mechanic, Tom encouraged himself; but after half a mile the risk of premature coronary and the fact that the car was no longer in sight inclined him to call off the experiment.

Slowing down to a canter, Tom continued into the town, past closed garages and pubs, past Ellard's fish and chip shop abandoned to its smell, trotting through this town already shut up for the night, like some health freak jogging, hearing the clip of his shoes on the pavement, seeing the lights in the shop windows snap off; and if people were watching, which they weren't, they'd be wrong to think this running was to exercise the heart, though it was badly bruised and in need of treatment, for if you ran long enough you could convince yourself that the heavy breathing was caused by the running and not by the thought of R.G. inviting himself into her flat, or the memory of her shorn head, or of that oaf Peter /Nick Ainsworth laying his hands on her, and your thoughts came without decoration, swelling as the air ripped out of your head, big thoughts, simple, complete:

Women are strange creatures.
But there's one you know who isn't.
She isn't the right one.
She is. Now.
You don't know what you want.
I do. And now.

'I was just off to bed. Hell, you are in a lather,' Liz said.

'Been running.'

'What for?'

'Give you these.'

'Crikey! It's gone midnight!'

'Best time.'

'Novel, anyway. Come to think of it, so are flowers, for me.'

'That's why.'

'Say it with flowers, eh?'

'No other way,' intent on sucking in breath.

'I like it,' referring to the occasion. 'They look a bit clapped out.'

'Like me.'

'You'd better come in and get your puff back.'

'Thanks.' Standing in the hall, he panted, 'Collapsed lung.'

'Want a bicycle pump?'

'Just massage.'

'You should've kept away from Gritley Thespians. The drama's catching.'

'Didn't you go? I didn't see you.'

'I was backstage. Where've you been, then? You're all wet.'

'It must be from the flowers,' he answered, looking down at his trousers. Damp had taken over most of the

131

fabric covering his thighs, spotted with chlorophyll like green mould. 'I wanted to keep them fresh.'

'Dry cleaning's the best thing for freshening up trousers. You'd better take them off. I'll find something else.'

One thing he appreciated about Liz was her direct approach. No complexities. Straight in. He hadn't been in the house three minutes and she'd got his trousers off. That might well deserve a mention in the *Guinness Book of Records*. The only thing that puzzled him was how she knew what he had come for.

Waiting for her, Tom examined his legs. He considered that they were not at all bad. They not only conformed to the standard model but they had optional extras such as a discreet suggestion of muscle, shape and a considerable growth of hair. The whole effect would be better, of course, without socks and shoes. As he removed them, he was reminded that the quality control supervisor at Sweeter Feet had not yet sent a replacement.

From the twitch of her nostrils, he deduced that Liz resisted her impulse to compliment the exposed limbs as she handed him a dressing gown. 'This'll keep your bum warm,' was all she allowed herself. 'Don left it. But it comes in.'

It had come in for quite a lot. One pocket was half off; the belt carriers were torn; the braid had left its mooring in places and hung in dejected loops. Wearing a dressing gown was a more strenuous occupation than he had imagined.

'We might as well have a drink while your trousers dry. I've some home-made. Don't worry, I didn't make it! Stan's. Can't do with the fuss.'

She flicked a couple of glasses through the stagnant

suds in the sink, withdrew a bottle from one of the open cartons, and grappled with the cork. Following her into the living room, he watched as she knelt on the rug and rattled coals into the grate.

It was disappointing that she had kept her dress on. He thought of suggesting that she follow the old cliché and slip into something more comfortable, but the remark might be regarded as premature. Anyway, at least he was dressed for the part, better than Peter. Silk would have been more classy, but you had to adapt, so he tucked a hand in the torn pocket and made a few elegant paces across the room.

'For heaven's sake, stop poncing about,' Liz interrupted him. 'Have a drink.'

Sometimes her matter-of-fact tendency could be discouraging. He wondered what Peter would have said.

'Do women wear garters nowadays?' he asked.

The question amused her. She spluttered, spraying out wine. 'You doing market research? Occasionally, I suppose. But not me. Can't even stand tights.' Using the hem of her dress to dab her chin, she revealed her freedom from hose and its accessories. Tom found it necessary to take a quick turn round the furniture.

'Not a bad little wine,' he finally ventured.

This time Liz had none in her mouth, so her response was less messy. 'It's foul,' she managed at last. 'Last year's old boots. A bit much, at the end of the day when I'm tired, like now. So probably be sloshed quick. Have another. A goblet full of the warm south.'

'Beaker,' he corrected.

'How d'you mean, beaker? That's a glass.'

'The line is, "Oh, for a beaker full of the warm south".'

'Who says?'

'Keats.'

'He should have said goblet. It's better. That's what is the matter with you, Tom.'

'I'm not saying I like beaker more. It just happens to be the right word.'

'That's what I mean. It doesn't always do.'

He decided that this was not the moment to enter into controversy. You cannot alter habits of illogical thinking in a few brisk minutes.

'Won't you sit down, Tom? You make me nervous, going around fiddling.'

There was plenty of room beside her on the rug, a greying fleece removed late in life from a sheep suffering from alopecia and ticks, and bearing little resemblance to others he had come across. Even, so, it revived memories. He deemed it wiser to take up a position on the couch.

'That's better. Relax.'

'I'd feel more relaxed if you sat up here,' he said.

The suggestion was inspired but difficult to follow up. She had scrambled off the rug and settled down beside him, yet to put an arm round her straight away seemed unsubtle. He tried conversation while planning the next move.

'Did you make satisfactory progress with the set this evening?' he asked.

'Not bad. You sound like an end-of-term report! God, you kill me sometimes, Tom.' She leant quickly on to him and kissed him on the cheek. Though he was given no time to follow this up, he did contrive to get an arm round her waist. She made no comment, her attention suddenly taken by something floating in her glass.

'I don't like to tell him,' she commented, 'but Stan does make rotten wine. Needs a better sieve. You drink your bottles or sling them down the sink?'

'He's never given me one.'

'Not you, you nit.'

'Mike hasn't mentioned it.'

She turned and examined him carefully. 'You're a sweetie,' she pronounced. 'And so innocent. Sometimes I wonder how you manage.'

He winced. 'You've said something like that before. I suppose Stan could have given Belinda a bottle. He does drop in.'

'Hell, I shouldn't have said. It's the drink talking. Forget it. But you needn't worry. She's not really interested in Stan, the poor sod.'

It took Tom several minutes to understand. During which, his face registered perplexity, incredulity, then astonishment.

'Damn. I shouldn't have said,' Liz repeated.

So it was *Belinda* that Stan fancied! 'I thought he was after Jonquil,' Tom gasped.

'Not him.'

He wanted explanations. (How could Stan go for Belinda? The man must be bonkers.) But before coherence returned, Liz continued, 'You still interested in her, then?'

'Off and on,' he answered absently, trying to recall why he had misinterpreted Stan's behaviour: offering a daily joinery service, borrowing books, being cautioned that indiscretions were better conducted t'other side of the Pennines.

'Only off and on?' Liz demanded.

Tom realized that consideration of this news was distracting him from his purpose. Neither did he wish to discuss Jonquil at that particular moment. So he shrugged. 'She's a very elusive woman.'

Which was not the epithet you would apply to Liz. It

was unlikely that you had to chase her round the furniture. She was solid and would stay in one place. In fact, she was in rather a good place at that moment, viz, inside the crook of his arm and pressing against his chest.

'I've told you what to do about that. Have you taken my advice?'

'I tried.'

'How far did you get?'

He would not have imagined that reporting progress with one woman could nourish amorous notions in another, but with each question Liz squashed a little more of herself upon him.

'Not very far.'

'You should have grabbed harder.'

It then occurred to him that she was less interested in the application of her advice to Jonquil than to herself. He put down his glass and, after a few seconds' hesitation, cleared a space for his free hand. She wriggled under his touch.

'No need for you to have hang-ups about it. I reckon she knows her way around, from the look of her. Not like me. I was, what d'you call it? – a child bride. That's it. A child bride. Didn't know a thing.' Though drunkenness was fast overtaking her and hampering clear articulation, it did improve the flow. 'Consider you do, of course, but when it comes to it, you don't think. I wasn't any older than you when I had Sarah, but I don't mind now; she's a lovely baby. Funny, when you think of it. I wouldn't have her if I'd paid more attention.'

'You certainly made up for it afterwards.' He had a new problem now, not one of contact – there was quite a lot of that – but of how to stop Liz talking. While she continued, her mouth remained inaccessible.

136

'You can say that again. And do you know, for a bit I was so scared of falling for another, I'd have the Pill and spermicides and just to make sure, him in a sheath!'

'You mean Don?'

'Not him! He took fright as soon as he saw the baby. Some men are like that. Mind you, she did look a bit off.'

'Who, then?' He was beginning to appreciate why she had been interested in Jonquil; the effect of discussing another person in a similar situation was astonishing. Also, there was her hand, no longer encumbered by the glass, roving about inside Don's gown.

'Whoever it was. What you take me for? Are you planning to turn celibate at twenty?'

At this rate, Tom moaned silently, he would never be anything else.

'Mind you,' Liz continued relentlessly, 'it's not as easy as you might think. When you're by yourself, some men think all they have to do is nod and, Geronimo, they're on. Expect you're always available. So I make sure I don't give them ideas, 'less I want. And give them no reason to think they've done me a good turn. Keep independent. That's the best way.'

All this confiding had begun to tire her. She laid her head on his shoulder but it was still impossible to reach her mouth. He stroked her hair.

'There's lots of different sorts,' she murmured, her lips wet against his throat. 'Some reckon they're doing you a favour – you know, the frustrated woman, needing a man – when all they want is a good time, easy. Then there's others that don't pretend but still reckon they're an offer you can't refuse. And then there's them that think you're just there for their convenience. A public convenience.' She sniggered.

137

'I don't think you're right about that, Liz,' he said carefully. It was strange how the room had suddenly gone cold.

'That's because you are sweet,' she answered, her fingers stroking his chest, tweaking the hairs. That hurt now. 'I know I'm right. There are some around with problems they think they can sort out with a quick lay. Therapy. Think everything will be O.K. if they can just get it out of their system.' She giggled coarsely, coughed and fell silent.

It was the moment he had been planning for, but he could not now put it to use. He waited until she was asleep then he lifted her away from him, rose, and gently arranged her along the couch. As he laid Don's dressing gown over her, a note fell from the corner of the hanging pocket. 'For Liz. Enjoy a goblet full of the warm south, or anyway, warm Yorkshire. Perhaps, in time, my thanks will be more adequate.'

Tom looked down at Liz and bent to pick a piece of fluff out of her hair. This lover did not fall into any of her categories and in spite of her tipsy garrulity she had kept him secret. It was not hard to imagine why.

He stooped over her. Seeing her like this, it was easy to imagine her tender, sympathetic with a man who desired, pretty hopelessly, another woman; up to a point, she had been that with him, Tom; but she had not given also her love. That she reserved for Stan.

Tom kissed her and pulled the dressing gown over her throat. No wonder Stan was grateful. Though admitting to her what he felt about Belinda, he could find affection with Liz. He had not been dishonest; she would not allow that.

It would be fine to have someone like that around, Tom thought. And tried to silence the regret.

Chapter Eleven

Tom unscrewed his pen, removed the cartridge, smelt it, licked it, shook it against his ear, then replaced it. The present essay was not going very well: 'Comment on the Wife of Bath's Prologue as a satire on marriage'. In fact, if you chose to be pedantic, you could say that it was not going at all. Pedantic was the epithet he had applied to Olly Hardy when he had renewed his demands to share Tom's thoughts on various literary topics. Olly Hardy had not only felt unable to accept the word as a suitable description but had refused to allow Tom in his class until he had given in the last essay set, plus all the back numbers for the term. Since by now the whole series ran to six, Tom had attempted some last-minute negotiation.

'You'll turn me into a hack,' he had accused.

Olly had indicated that he was prepared to take that risk.

That was Monday, the beginning of a pulverizing week.

Tom looked at the empty sheet of paper in front of him. Over the last three days he had written four essays. That worked out at an average per day of one point three three recurring. There must be more interesting ways of employing one's time. Also, he could do with a little therapy; getting the events of the week down on paper might exorcize them from his mind. He drew the sheet towards him and headed it 'Notes for the Autobiography of Thomas Taylor, second volume, A Seminal Adolescence.'

Tuesday: Kate's manner icy, but she did lapse into conversation for a couple of sentences, the sort you can do without. 'I understand that you kept your appointment with Julia. A pity it was such a waste of time.' And a pity, too, that she couldn't be more original. It was the popular interpretation of the action going on in the common room, i.e. Julia performing her scenes with Neville, plus others not mentioned in the text. No one left in any doubt about her change of affections. A good many glances, checking my reaction. Felt humiliated. Could hardly stop the show and shout that they'd got it all wrong. In the bog, Pin tried to commiserate. 'You can't win them all. How was you to know that she is into West Indians?'

Wednesday: Bumped into Stan coming out of the English stockroom. 'Can I help you?' I asked, as if I owned the place. 'No, thanks,' says he. 'Just returning a book.' (Seems to be something of a reader. Always returning books, or intending to. But skims, hence goblet for beaker.) I was ready for a chat. It's lonely, sweating for hours over essays. Also, I thought a few well-chosen words might cheer Stan up; he was looking distinctly low. I felt sorry for him. It must be appalling to fancy a woman like my mother! 'Belinda liked your idea for filling in that gap behind the new sink unit,' I said by way of encouragement. 'Did she?' he said. 'I dropped in Friday after I'd been to Gritley but she wasn't at home.' 'She'd taken Dave Aspinall into Leeds, to a Writers' Circle. You know he writes? She's giving him a bit of help.' He looked more low after I'd mentioned Dave, so I added, 'I shouldn't worry about

Dave. He's not likely to be much competition.' 'Competition? What do you mean by that?' It was then that I realized that perhaps I'd gone too far. That's the trouble with some people, offer sympathy and they become resentful. 'Just an expression,' I tried to shrug it off, but he was beginning to look pedantic. 'Don't think I'm criticizing, Stan, only remember you did pass a comment once about indiscretions.' 'And you think I'm engaged in one?' I would have liked to mention that I regarded Belinda as less of an indiscretion than a disaster, but he didn't give me the chance. That pedantic look had turned nasty. 'Been watching, have you? Think you've seen a few signs?' (*Me*, see a few signs! If it hadn't been for Liz I would never have known!) 'My God! What you suffer from is an overheated imagination.' He was shouting by this time. 'It takes two to make an indiscretion, my lad, and I can tell you here and now that there aren't that number in any you may be thinking of. And another thing. You may learn, one day, that indiscretion also means being foolhardy enough to let your affection light on someone out of reach. It's not only hopping into bed, you filthy-minded little prick.' He didn't have to swing his fist. I had already taken that one on the chin.

16.00 hours. Accepted a lift from R.G., hoping for a little gossip on unstressful subjects. Unfortunately, R.G. did not share my inclinations. 'Haven't seen you all day, Tom. Someone said Olly had done a good butcher's job and was sporting your guts. Sorry about that. Also about Julia. Try not to take it too hard. She's only interested in the theatre and anyone who can give her a leg-up has got a head start. (R.G. never worries about metaphors.) 'And this guy Neville is already at drama school. Fenton's arranged rehearsals of his scenes at

141

weekends when he can chug up in his banger. Being a drama student adds to his glamour, which one would think, looking at him, he has enough of without. Anyway, if you feel like drowning your sorrows, just give me a ring.

'Speaking personally for a moment, last Friday turned out quite nicely for me,' R.G. prattled on. 'Thanks for putting Jonquil in my way. I'm surprised I hadn't noticed her before — must be getting slack. But I made up for it. She's very friendly and easy to get on with. And a nice little place she's got there.'

She had invited R.G. up to her flat! I spent all evening going over the routine — carafe of wine, cushions on carpet, shaded lamps. Only I didn't figure in the scenario and I could think of no way of writing myself in. The lover's brain is fertile with schemes and plots. But mine was arid. Dried up. Perhaps I should have plugged it with Oasis.

I wish she hadn't known about that. Going to flower arranging classes, a woman like her! Still, you couldn't expect her to be perfect. The lover loves the woman with all her faults, I told myself, trying to forget her answers to the questionnaire, the way she had let that oaf Nick Ainsworth grope for her garter, the way she had laughed with R.G. The trouble was, the arrangement was not reciprocal. Jonquil was indifferent despite my good points. I tried to make a list but couldn't think of any, off hand; a good indication of the state of my morale.

As Wednesday was finally crawling into Thursday, I found myself in the bathroom. I stood around for a while, hoping that an excuse for getting back into that flat would present itself. (I hadn't noticed her before . . . But I made up for it.) However, nothing came. No sudden blast. No mind-blowing inspiration. Picking up the toothpaste, I caught sight of a piece of paper attached by sellotape to Mike's can of shaving foam. Belinda's latest missive. I've added it to the file. 'Tom, though I applaud your shaving so frequently, I cannot stock the amount of soap you require since I do not visit the pharmacist daily. Will you, therefore, purchase the stuff yourself?' A clever move. My services were being extended to include shopping.

I pulled the note from the tin and wrote on the back: 'Dear Mum, I appreciate your encouragement and, indeed, your example to acquire a clean shave, but I have decided to grow a beard. Yours in love and understanding, your very own son, Tom.'

Replacing my pen in my pocket, I felt an obstruction, Liz's packet of Durex, complete except for a couple of practice samples. (Nice little place she's got there.) I added a postscript to my note. 'Since you cannot get to the chemist every day, you may find yourself running short. Please accept these with my compliments.' Then I taped the packet and the note to the can and went to bed. End of a rotten day.

Thursday: The first thought you have when waking is supposed to be the last one you had before going to sleep, so mine was no different from usual. As usual, I went over the ground, modifying one detail, that cape of black hair. Second thought was that I'd give school a miss; I didn't think I was up to weaving a path round Stan, Julia, Kate and R.G. At home, I'd be out of their reach. Nor should I be harassed by Belinda; that was the fate of her F.E. classes at this time of the week. Which brought me to thought number three: that small gift to her had not been well chosen. I scurried into the bathroom, bent on retrieval, but Belinda had reached it first. Or Mike. I could hear them downstairs.

When I joined them the atmosphere was heavy. I'm good at sensing that sort of thing. Mike was annihilating cornflakes between nutcracker molars and the *Guardian* was still unfolded at Belinda's elbow. I tried to introduce a little light relief by asking them if they were interested in the Special Cut-Out Play-a-Joke Family Game on the back of the cereal packet but they were unresponsive.

'We have received a letter from Mr Childe,' Mike announced, fingering sheets headed with the familiar crest. 'Apparently your work has been very unsatisfactory this term. In fact, non-existent. Everyone who teaches you agrees on this, except one who claims you have made, I quote, some innovative contributions in peer-group situations which indicate a stabilizing value system when confronting issues of socio-ethical dimension, unquote.' Mike had a hard job with that. 'A Mr Goodenough. You may have met him. Fortunately, I haven't. I hope my luck holds.' He then returned to Nanny's three-page treatise. 'It also appears that you absent yourself from lessons to such an extent that many of the staff were incredulous on learning that you are still, technically at least, a pupil of the school. Next,' he continued, summarizing the paragraphs, 'the deterioration in your work is not only disappointing in view of your attainment in the Lower Sixth but occasions anxiety about university entrance on which you continually evade Mr Childe. He points out that a decision must be made within the next week. He ventures to inquire whether you are under any physical or emotional stress and ends by trusting that I and, indeed, my good wife, will give careful consider-

144

ation to his letter and, together with him, bring about that improvement which is so desirable and which must be our aim.'

Silence. Mike is good at that and Belinda was leaving the interview to him. When it suits her, she lets Women's Liberation nod off. 'Nanny certainly spreads himself,' I commented. 'Yes, I agree. I could have got that on a memo the size of a postage stamp: Your son is a dosser wasting his time and the staff's. Please see that this is corrected forthwith.' 'I think he exaggerates,' I tried. 'Just exaggerates?' I had never seen Mike so angry. 'How exaggerated is it? Perhaps we should go through it systematically. Do you ever cut lessons?'

So the interrogation progressed and by the time he had finished I was in an advanced state of shock. I sent up a little prayer of thanks that I was not one of his employees.

'Since you say you still want to go to university, you make your choices by Sunday evening,' he ordered, 'then I will telephone Mr Childe. Now,' he went on, checking the agenda, 'we come to his charitable explanations for your conduct. One, that you are ill. I can arrange for a medical check.' I managed to indicate that one was not necessary. 'Very well. That brings us to his suspicion of emotional stress. I can't say that I've noticed any myself but I have a high tolerance for lunatic behaviour which may be due to hereditary characteristics for which I am partly responsible. Having said that, I am left with only one explanation: a girl.'

We faced each other across the table. I came out of shock. 'I'm not prepared to comment on that. It's none of your business,' I answered him. 'This letter makes it my business.' It was my turn to be silent. 'Look, Tom,

I'm not asking for dates and times and vital statistics or suggesting you put her on ice till after A-levels, but don't you think your handling of the business is rather extreme?' 'I can't claim to be handling it at all.' 'So I gather. Oh God, isn't life bloody?' We were back on the old terms. 'Tom, you'll have to get down to some work, see her less often, make the occasions when you do more special. Whatever I mean by that! But for heaven's sake, cooperate, will you?' 'I've been working all week on essays for Olly Hardy,' I told him, which was more or less true.

After that they both rushed off. I declined Mike's offer of a lift into school on the grounds that I needed the exercise and retired to my bachelor's quarters. I felt guilty about that since Mike had been so reasonable, but I couldn't face Life Outside. However, retirement was not the solution. Nanny had reached me by using the post. That should have warned me. It didn't. So I was unprepared when I answered the telephone at half past four.

'Tom Taylor?' the voice said. 'I'm Julian Marshall, Julia's father.' I had already decided that I did not like the sound of him. 'I was given to understand that last Friday evening Julia and yourself were engaged on research for a paper on the Women's Liberation Movement.' 'That's right.' 'Did this occupy you the whole of the evening?' 'Well, it is a very big subject.' 'Precisely. That is why I am surprised that you had time to travel to the Gritley Thespians. In view of the fact that I had expressly forbidden Julia to engage in amateur theatricals this year, I regard your encouragement as intolerable interference in my parental authority.' 'Julia doesn't need me to encourage her.' 'I prefer to accept my daughter's word on that. I also prefer her not to be associated with a young man of such dubious character that he arrives at a theatre violently demanding a part, interrupts a rehearsal, abandons my daughter to be brought home by a total stranger and runs amok, breaking light bulbs and stealing flowers. I have spoken to Mrs Maud Cockcroft and Mr Fenton Strachan and they have informed me of this. They also report that you are a rabid racist, objecting to a West Indian whose part you hoped to snatch, and publicly rude to a young man called Trevor whom you accused of being a queer. Though you anticipated my own objections to these two, I want to put it on record that I take strong exception to your assuming the right to speak for me. It is I, not you, who decides whom Julia shall meet. However, Mr Strachan assures me that the West Indian is an up-and-coming young man in the London theatre and that in the future we shall all be proud to claim his acquaintance, so I am prepared to make an exception. He also assures me that acting in *A Touch of Honey* will be of great value to Julia in her English examinations. Therefore I have agreed to let her continue. My reason for telephoning was to let you know that I am writing to your headmaster to inform him that he harbours in his sixth a vandal, a thief and an evil subversive who persuades young girls to flout their father's authority. Since you claim that you were engaged upon research with Julia last Friday evening, I shall add the name of liar to that list. Good day.'

Friday: Got up, eventually. Endured Belinda's nagging that I'd be late for school. Returned to solitary confinement after she had left. Wrote this. So far today, Life Inside has been tranquil, by which I mean that Life Outside has left me alone.

*

Tom clipped the sheets together and went downstairs to make a cup of coffee. When the telephone rang he did not answer it immediately. He was not going to listen to further insults from Julia's monstrous father. Finally, the noise won.

'I don't want to hear any more of your obscene abuse, you thundering great turd,' he shouted into the mouthpiece.

'Have you been having that kind of call? I thought they always chose women. What do they say?'

'Dave! I assumed it was Julia's father again.'

'Again? I didn't know you had struck up a friendship with him. Is Belinda in?'

He noticed the ease with which Dave gave her name. 'She teaches all day Thursday and Friday. Can I give her a message?'

'No, thanks. I just wanted a word.'

There was a pause. It seemed that Tom was no substitute.

'I've gone into retirement this week.' Tom prompted solicitous inquiry.

'Why's that?'

He wished Dave could sound more concerned. 'Burrowing underground. Licking the sores.'

That raised a flicker of interest. 'Anything to do with Julia and her violent change of affection?'

'Not really.' He would have liked to tell him. He was tired of going through it, over and over again, with himself. It was the first time since it had started that he had felt like that. It showed how much he had missed chewing the cud with Dave. 'I'll tell you some time. How's everything there?' Dave was calling from the school phone.

'The day has had its moments. Goodenough is wearing Ellard's donkey jacket, emblazoned with orange plastic. Thus decked out, he began his lesson by rabbiting on about decay in moral standards. It was his marriage guidance bit, you know the routine. You'd have liked it, but Kate took offence. In fact, she went completely ape over what she declared were his insinuations and walked out. Can you believe that?

'I suspect that something is wrong there. She's been going around looking absolutely foul. Grey face, pinched lips, furrowed brow, bowed shoulders. I thought I ought to slip in a discreet inquiry, but saw R.G. with her, so tackled him. He said, better to leave it alone for the time being. What do you make of that? Anyway, what time did you say Belinda would be back?'

'I didn't.'

'Do you know if she liked the flowers?'

'So you are responsible for these bewildered blooms that look like displaced persons among my mother's litter! She didn't say.'

'Didn't she?'

He sounded miserable, so Tom did not mention that he had assumed the flowers were a gift from Stan Driffield. Less charitably, he omitted to report that Belinda had spent some minutes drooling over them in an infantile way as she rammed them into a vase — clearly she had given flower arrangement classes a miss — because Dave had had the wine bar bit, hadn't he? What more did he want?

'How's the book?'

'Getting on.'

'You haven't told me yet what it's about. Usually you give me a rundown on the plot, at least.'

'It's rather awkward. I don't think I can explain at the

moment, Tom.' Then suddenly he cleared his throat and added, 'Hell, what's the odds? I expect you are bound to find out some time. It's about a young feller who's hot on a woman older than himself.'

Tom gasped. For a moment the walls spun. Then he shouted. 'Thanks. That's all I needed. I might have known you'd be on to it, somehow. Well, I'm warning you – just keep your bloody pen out of my life, you dirty little shit,' and slammed down the phone.

So Dave had found out and was making a book about it. Tom kicked each rise on the stairs as he went back to his room. But there must be some way of preventing an author from putting you into print. Not, of course, that any of Dave's rotten efforts reached that stage, but one just might now, with Belinda's help. That suggested another ghastly possibility: that she knew, too. They would enjoy discussing him and Jonquil, knocking back the vino in wine bars and champing through the management's special menu of the day. He had not imagined that, when he had encouraged Dave to approach her. But he might have guessed that she would get her own back, somehow.

'It was then, his fortunes at their lowest ebb, that Thomas Taylor came close to despair,' Tom attempted therapy as he pulled on a sweatshirt. 'He was abandoned by all; there was no one in whom he could trust,' sniffing at his socks. 'Even his closest friend had betrayed him, abetted by the wanton female who in a slack moment had given him birth,' lacing up his training shoes. 'One last resort remained to him. He would remove all vestiges of his existence from their ken. Not idly did he toy with the thought of emigration, but reluctantly he put that aside. No vast unexplored reaches of the world remained in which he could stride, unknown and unchallenged, nursing his pain. He therefore, as many a lover before him, chose another path. He girded up his loins, took one last look at the scene of his childhood and vanished into the mists of the moor.'

Few people witnessed his flight. A neighbour looked at him, surprised that he was not in school, and went indoors to telephone the talking clock. Avoiding the centre of the town, Tom cut through side-streets, snickets, laboured up flights of mossed steps and paths greasy with mud and a skin of fallen leaves. When he reached the moor he stumbled up a rutted track, turned off and began to scramble over boulders shelving across the course of a small frothing gill. Above was a spinney of Scots pine, his goal. Pausing for breath, he glanced up.

A figure stood under the trees, its back towards him, hands inside pockets of a coat whose skirt lifted and billowed in the wind. It could be Jonquil, he said to himself, left school early, having no lesson last period, and fitting in a healthy turn on the moor. Stan had said she liked outdoor exercise. Let it be Jonquil, he prayed. It was time he had a break. However she greeted him, he must not let this opportunity pass. He would tell her outright how he felt.

It was quicker to thrust up the cleft of the spilling gill. Water soaked into his shoes; jutting rocks jabbed at his feet; slats of stone tilted and pinched his ankles; sharp flints massed under his scraping nails as he slithered and plunged, pulling himself up with his hands, his body spread-eagled across foam and boulders, ungainly in his haste. He must get to the spinney before she had time to leave it, striding away from him over the ledge of the moor. If she did that, it would mean that she wished to avoid him, and he would not follow her. If she remained, she would be indicating that she would listen.

He looked up and saw that she was still there. The last few feet were taken with a force that dislodged barriers, sent rocks thudding and threw him down at the summit on hands and knees.

'Hello,' he called, as he pushed himself upright.

She turned. 'Are you training for something? Or just trying to impress?' Kate asked.

Chapter Twelve

Dignity runs short when water is dripping down your trousers and topping up your sodden shoes, and Tom observed that she was laughing. The last person he would have chosen to witness his frantic ascent was Kate.

'I thought you were someone else,' he explained.

Her face sobered. 'Oh, I didn't flatter myself that you had taken to scaling waterfalls for me. Please don't let me keep you. Feel free to piss off.'

'I am thinking of that,' he answered, squelching an experimental pace or two. He bent down and tweaked the fabric of his trousers. There was a sucking sound as it came away from his leg. It was clear that he had found a substitute for that polythene film stuff – Taylor's Trouser Wrap for preserving your cheese and fresh veg.

'Not a suitable costume for paddling,' Kate said, amused.

'They'll soon dry off.' Except today there was no dressing gown on offer while he waited, and Kate was no Liz. Looking back, he thought it was strange that he had been the one to take his clothes off. He had always imagined it was the other way round. 'All the same, some sympathy would be appreciated. I've had a heavy week.'

But with some women it was no use appealing to their softer instincts. If they had any, they made sure they did not waste them on him. 'Do you wonder?' she asked. 'You should have thought of that probability before you started.'

'Started what?' he demanded warily.

'Tangling with someone like Julia – ignoring homework, skipping lessons.'

She had not mentioned Jonquil. More relaxed, he said, 'I'm not the only one missing lessons at the moment.'

'So you've noticed?'

'Lay off for once, can't you, Kate? Whenever we are together, you move into attack. I don't know why.'

'No, I don't suppose you do.' She turned her head and stared at the town below them.

That was the sort of answer that was capable of transforming him from a sexual democrat into a raving male chauvinist. It implied that Kate had some special knowledge, and managed to reproach him for not having it while making no attempt to enlighten him.

'I don't see how you can expect me to guess. What's bugging you, Kate?'

'You actually want to know? Well, I've had a heavy week as well – several, in fact.'

'Dave telephoned this lunchtime and said you had walked out of Goodenough's lesson. Created quite a sensation. He also said that you weren't looking so good. And you aren't, Kate, looking at you.'

'Well, thanks. For looking, I mean.' She brushed fir cones aside and sat down.

'You ill?'

'No, this isn't supposed to be an illness.'

She sat with her back straight, her look bridging the town and moving backwards and forwards across the opposite moor, while her fingers picked at a dry cone.

Tom was puzzled. 'I don't follow.'

'My God! For someone who's supposed to be bright, you're bloody dense, Tom!'

'And for someone who claims to prefer straight talk, you're bloody enigmatic.'

'You can be so naive! After what I've just said, and you still haven't got it!'

Tom tried to reconstruct the conversation. Unfortunately, there seemed no rational sequence. He told her so.

She shrugged.

'Look, one minute you accuse me of being dense, and the next you rebuff me when I am trying to understand. You want it both ways. Quite honestly, Kate, it's impossible to talk to you.'

He stopped, surprised by his anger, surprised to hear that he had shouted, surprised to find that he was kneeling beside her, gripping her arm. She did not flinch. Neither did anger flare in answer to his.

'That's because it is so complicated,' she said. 'It's all mixed up. I can't stop thinking about it. Not only about the thing itself, but how it happened. If I explained, you'd say that I was trying to involve you. I'm not. It's entirely my own fault.'

Her face was grey. The words grated out. He saw her effort to maintain coherence. Tom lent into her and again the scent of her hair eluded him, but it seemed that, if he got closer, he might discover what it was. 'But I don't mind being involved,' he told her.

She shook her head, her eyes on the bald ridges above the layered town. Then abruptly her body sagged. She swung away and rolled sideways upon the litter of fronds and twigs, and before her shoulders were twitched with suppressed sobs, she whispered, 'You see, I think I'm pregnant.'

155

Her mouth was turned aside from him, pressed into the damp moss.

Tom had no idea how long he sat there after Kate scrambled up, apologized, said that she did not want to discuss it, that she had had enough for one day, and went home alone.

The slopes of the moor folded upon him, dark at his shoulder; below, the lamps of the town spangled the rising night. He shivered. His trousers were damp; his shoes sodden. Still crouched by the place where Kate had whispered, he looked down at the houses edging the moor, saw lights switched on in a room he had once entered, made out two figures, and rose, too weary to ponder on whom Jonquil had invited back to her flat.

'Vinegar?' Ellard asked, poised with the bottle.

'No, thanks. I'll eat them at home.'

'They say it's good for the you-know-what. Cheaper than oysters.'

'You've got a dirty mind, Ellard.'

'It don't stop at my mind, either. And who's talking? I'll never forget you a fortnight back at Reg Grimshaw's party, all over that Julia like boobs was going out of fashion, make anyone blush. Couldn't fancy her myself. Still, it takes all sorts. Meant to ask how you got on.'

'You needn't bother.'

'Like that, was it? Not having any, was she, when it came to it? I'm not surprised.'

'No! But I'd rather not talk about it. I'm thinking of her.'

'There is that. I mean, if she's got style, you'd be daft to spread it around. Don't do to invite competition.'

'I don't know how you manage to work in this place, Ellard. The smell makes me sick.'

'Don't notice it. Here.' He opened the packet and added another piece of fried fish. 'That's on the house. I'll never forget you, pissed out of your mind, going over that sweatshirt for pockets – ever so helpful, you were – all set to lend me a couple of rubber johnnies. Which you hadn't got.'

There is much to discourage a lover, Tom said to himself as he plodded home. Disappointments are many. He suffers slumps in fortune. Soulless observers are affronted by his passion and object to his necessary schemes. All this is part of his training and he endures it without complaint. But there are other parts less easy to deal with. Thought, for one. Previously kept exclusively for his mistress, it can become subject to unpredicted distractions.

Kate.

It was ironic that it should be Kate. And now Ellard. Who went for girls with style. Who was at R.G.'s party. Tom shuddered. He felt like a voyeur. But he wanted to know.

'I'd like a word, if you can spare a minute,' he told Belinda. 'Or are you dashing off for a candle-lit gossip in a flesh-pot in Leeds?' It was essential not to slacken. The opposition was not having it all its own way.

'Not tonight. There was no need for the fish and chips. Didn't you see my note?'

'Which one? You scatter them so liberally, one can get ignored. That's the risk when you go in for overkill.'

'I said there is a pizza you can put under the grill. I haven't the energy to prepare anything more complicated after a day's teaching.'

It was really impressive how she managed to imply that every other day of the week she produced elaborate dishes, certified Cordon Bleu. 'I think I'll stick to fish and chips. Would you like a piece of fish, though I'm afraid it's not up to wine-bar standard?'

'I hesitate to take the food out of my child's mouth.'

Tom could appreciate her scruples as they examined the rectangles of batter.

'Give yourself a break, Belinda. Stop toiling over a hot cooker and enjoy yourself. Free, too. Ellard Richardson's special. On the house.'

As she took a piece, Tom awarded her a mark for not being pedantic about Ellard's hand-out. 'Know anything about pregnancy?' he asked.

'Only by hearsay. Your birth came as a complete surprise,' performing a caesarian section upon the bloated fish.

There were moments when she reminded him of Kate. Why was it his fate to be the whetstone for such women?

'Look, Belinda, I do know the obvious points. They filter through to the male consciousness. But what about the symptoms? Do they affect women straight away?'

'It depends.'

If you were not pressed for time and had plenty of stamina, you could rely on Belinda for comprehensive information, though it was necessary to accept a certain school-marmy idiom that invaded her style, deal with a finger wagged in your face, and ignore the spray as excitement in her subject stimulated the ageing glands. By the end of fifteen minutes, Tom had been conducted over the whole course from morning sickness to the first contraction. He eyed the congealed chips on his plate and told himself that he had not been very interested in them in the first place.

'Thanks, Belinda. But how is it that a woman can only think she is pregnant?'

He realized immediately that the question was too particular and it was an effort to remain composed under her stare. That was the trouble with women, he groaned to himself: they cannot keep a discussion objective; sooner or later they will make it personal. Struggling on, he explained, 'I mean, she can suppose she is, from the usual indications, but isn't there any way of her being sure? There's a urine test or something, isn't there?'

There was. You could send a specimen through the post; or you could take it along to a clinic; or you could hand it over the counter of a pharmacist advertising the service. One important detail he had to remember was that it should be an early-morning sample, because a richer potion sophisticated with orange juice, Alka-Seltzer or the breakfast cuppa would affect the result. Tom took the point, You could not have postmen, lab assistants and pharmacists pissed out of their minds at the first sniff. Also, there were the home kits. But you could not depend on them. Because of the human element.

Before he could observe that it might be difficult to eliminate the human element in urine, Belinda had resumed her stare and was homing in. 'Tom, why all these questions? Are you trying to tell me something?'

'No, Mum. I'm feeling fine. No lethargy. No varicose veins. No tender nipples. No back ache. No morning sickness. Everything absolutely normal.'

'And what about the girl?'

'Girl? Oh, I get you. You think there's a girl?'

'Pregnancy is generally a female condition.'

'But you aren't suggesting that a man cannot be interested in it, are you, Belinda? Thanks to you, my formative years have been devoted to relieving

159

the plight of women, with special reference to yours.'

'It would have been more to the point if you had prevented her getting into such a plight,' she took him up smartly, 'rather than boning up on it afterwards.'

It was the moment for complete denial and careful correction. Tom missed it. When warming to a subject, Belinda could talk without pause for breath.

'You may be my son,' preferring to retain a degree of doubt about the relationship, 'but my first concern is with the girl.'

As she went on, Tom encouraged himself with the thought that Belinda was referring to a girl, not a woman. Presumably when she and Dave had been analysing his condition and working out its scope for a blockbusting novel, they had not included motherhood for Jonquil in the plot. It seemed that had been reserved for a girl of Tom's acquaintance. Tom reflected that, in the interest of Art, Belinda was prepared to envisage having a sex maniac for a son.

'It strikes me that your behaviour has been thoroughly irresponsible,' she was saying.

In the natural break that followed, Tom contrived to point out that his questions had arisen from a purely scientific interest.

'It is a pity that your commitment to science led you to such disastrous experiment,' she snapped. 'Please don't play games with me, Tom. Frankly, I did not find that packet of Durex much of a joke.'

Tom gasped. 'That was just a spontaneous gesture, Belinda.'

'And it was half empty, too. I concluded that you had finished with the girl and did not wish to be reminded of the incident. But I never imagined that you might

160

have dumped them because they were no longer any use!'

For Belinda a simple interpretation was never enough, Tom moaned to himself. That was one of the results of her addiction to literature. Encouraged by the stuff she read, she would always choose a complicated explanation for the most ordinary behaviour. He wondered momentarily whether he might have inherited the tendency.

'Belinda, will you please get it into your thick skull that I am not, repeat not, responsible for the pregnancy of anyone, man or woman.'

He could see that she was not convinced but could not bring herself to say so. Tom smiled at her. It was a shame having to reject her ingenious deductions. The woman looked quite miserable.

However, she rallied slightly as he rose from the table. 'Well, it is obvious that you are anxious, even if not responsible. By responsible, I mean directly. However, I hope you have a less limited notion of the word.'

'No need to moralize, Belinda. Any further postscript before we part?'

'Liz telephoned to ask if you could baby-sit this evening,' she answered wearily. 'She's helping with the set for *A Taste of Honey* at Gritley.'

'I know. Stan Driffield is in charge.'

'So I understand.' There was no sign of interest in how Stan occupied his leisure hours.

Since he had learnt that Stan was attracted to Belinda, Tom had tried to work out what he saw in her. With effort, it was possible to discern a few faint attributes that might induce an interest. Her face was not too bad, and she was not putting on weight, and when she unclipped her hair to fall on her shoulders, she looked quite young, considering. Some men might even go for her personality, a bit like Kate's, never letting up, always challenging. Mike had done so, once; in fact he still seemed to enjoy it. But marriage was a matter of adjustment and habit. Tom was pleased that, years before, he had decided against it.

However, it had some advantages. Unlike the lover, the husband had certain facilities. Bed, for one. And another thing, you could bet that few husbands stumbled in searching for their spouse and found themselves in the grip of a harpy like Julia. On their own hearthrug. Even if you tried to see the mistake from all angles, it was difficult to imagine any of them welcoming it.

The telephone rang as he left the kitchen. By now conditioned to break into a sweat at the sound, Tom slunk past and made for the stairs.

'For heaven's sake, answer it,' Belinda shouted.

'This is a telephone answering machine,' he croaked into the mouthpiece. 'When you hear the pips, will you please give your name and speak your message slowly.' Before he had got very far with the pips, R.G. said, 'If the machine's broken down, Tom, you might as well take the call yourself.'

'I expected it was Julia's father.'

'In that case, I understand. Having trouble there?'

'Dire. He's threatening to write to Flash Harry.'

'I shouldn't worry too much about that. It's his hobby. Once complained to Flash that I was escorting Julia home in Dad's car. Very worried about what it might lead to. Flash fetched me in, said he was obliged to take the matter up, and we talked it over. Flash was very interested. Said that in his job it was necessary to keep in touch.'

'Is there anything you cannot handle, R.G.?'

'Plenty. In fact, I'd say most of the important things, if I wanted to make myself miserable. You know what I'm talking about.' He was reminding Tom of his confession to Kate at the party.

'Yes, I know. But I think you are wrong there.'

'I'm not. Something has cropped up this week that shows that I'm right.'

'What has cropped up?'

'Better not say at present. Still, there's others in the same boat. Dave, for a start. But you'll know about that.'

'I don't. Haven't had a proper word for weeks.' Nor did he want one until he felt up to challenging Dave's right to put him in a book.

'He's gone on someone. Not that he says. I'm just reading the signs. It's all the rage, at the moment. Like a bug going round.' He paused, and Tom wondered whether he knew of Kate's suspected pregnancy. 'Even Julia gives the impression that she's serious about that guy Neville. There is the exception, though: Pin. He's sticking to computers. I tell him he ought to cash in on that – provide a dating service for the community. Thinking on, I recall why I have phoned. Jonquil Faulkner is throwing a party – tomorrow night – and wonders if you can come.'

Tom gripped the handset. He had the feeling that if he did not answer quickly the invitation would be withdrawn. 'Yes,' he managed. A monosyllable, but it exhausted his breath.

'Splendid. I thought that would suit. You see, I've been working it out. I thought I would like to know who had been giving my name to the secretaries so that Jonquil Faulkner would think I'd been after her address. So I had a little chat with a woman in the office, the one with the rattling dentures. Even then, it took me a bit to

163

work it out, after the way you had been carrying on with Julia, but in the end I got the message. I'm not so dim as folks think.'

'No one thinks you are.'

'You needn't start flattery, just because I've fixed you a date. I had to give Jonquil a hint, of course. I hope you don't mind. I couldn't let her continue to think that I was the one. It seemed like my main fascination, so it wasn't fair.'

'R.G.! I didn't think fairness came into it.'

'It wouldn't, believe me, if I went for her, but I don't. I like her, all right, but anyone more than a couple of years older than me doesn't turn me on, not permanent. But you rate her, then?'

'I rate her all right.' It was astonishing how easy it was to admit it. R.G.'s candour was infectious.

She had asked him to a party! He was on! Soft lights, intimate conversation, the freedom engendered by drink. He would have to be careful about that; the track record was poor. Though, with Julia, passing out had been a blessing. On the other hand, he could not have Jonquil lapsing into snores, like Liz. Not that he had been capable of much after what she had said. He liked Liz, and had wanted her by the end, but that was not how it had started. Disappointment over one woman is no reason for making love to another. Point taken.

Meanwhile, there was something he had to read up and he could not risk Belinda's catching him going through the bookshelves downstairs. Perhaps Liz had some books on it. He would have a look. It was lucky that he was baby-sitting this evening. After what Belinda had described, he didn't much like the idea of being pregnant.

'You in a lather again!' Liz greeted him. 'Good of you to come at such short notice. Sure you wouldn't rather be at the rehearsal?'

'No, I'm giving it a miss.'

'Thought you might be. Here,' she led him into the kitchen. 'Stan's in the front. You two fallen out?'

'You could say that.'

'That's the impression I got. Still, Stan's not a one to sulk. I'll put in a word.' She paused. Tom noticed that she looked tidier. There was no fluff in her hair. 'Sorry about last Friday night, Tom. Shouldn't have drunk so much. Had a few before I got in. But don't worry. I'll make up.'

'Not for that reason, Liz.'

'You're a sweetie.' She glanced down the hall, then bobbed up and kissed him. 'You're a real sweetie, you know that? Sorry we've got to go, but we're running late. Take time by the fetlock.'

'Forelock.'

'Wrong. The way I manage, it's practically past me before I can make a grab.'

Liz's reading matter was not extensive but spread around the house. However, he finally tracked down what he sought and though the books were soot-speckled and a little damp they were worth the effort. She had tackled the subjects of pregnancy, birth and child-rearing with the same thoroughness she had later applied to contraception. The collection would have filled a useful shelf in the public library, indeed part of it had once done so, since several volumes bore the local insignia and were stamped 'Reference'.

Carrying them into the front room, Tom built up the fire and settled down to read. After a couple of hours, he had to admit that Belinda had not exaggerated.

Embryology he could cope with, and illustrations of the foetus as it developed he found endearing, but the effects it could have on the mother made Tom feel sick. He could not imagine how women put up with it but, committed to his task he kept on, until, reaching the twentieth week of pregnancy, he began to feel movements inside his abdomen. Dismissing the alternatives of putting his feet up or practising sensible exercises, he went upstairs to the bathroom. Another dozen pages and he would be starting on the first contractions. A fellow needed a break.

The panel under the lip of the bath still gaped open and, stooping to press it back, he saw again Liz's booty from pharmacists and clinics. Recalling Jonquil's party the next day, he hesitated over a packet of Durex. It might be wise to go prepared, on the other hand he could easily nip into a chemist tomorrow. As he debated, he caught sight of a small carton that had not been there previously. Liz must have discovered a new device. You could rely on her to be in touch with the most recent developments.

Tom sat on the floor and opened it up. It was a do-it-yourself kit for testing pregnancy and held equipment for two goes. However, glancing through the accompanying leaflet, he could find no indication of what you concluded if the results were contradictory. To assume you were pregnant did not seem logical; on the other hand, it was not an issue susceptible to personal choice. Postponing that problem for a moment, he took out the plastic cylinder which held the two vials of liquid, two droppers, and two test-tubes each containing a small buff pellet. In other words, it had everything that was necessary, except that he was left to supply his own personal bit. Tom got up and went into the lavatory to extract it, first swilling out the tooth mug since lack of hygiene could produce a false result.

Back in the bathroom, he cleared a space on the floor and set up the experiment. Careful to follow the instructions exactly, he practised with one of the droppers until he had perfected the technique. This took some time and he had used up most of the mugful before he was satisfied. Wondering briefly where he had squirted it, he released two drops over the pellet at the bottom of the test-tube, broke a vial, added the liquid to the other ingredients, placed the bung in the test-tube, shook it in the manner directed and stood it in the holder. Underneath was a small mirror in which he would, after two hours, READ THE TEST RESULT.

While waiting, it was sensible to continue the research, but he felt nervous. Despite the fascination of the material in front of him, he kept glancing at his watch. Much more of this, he said to himself, and I shall be looking like Kate.

He was well into the section on spontaneous abortion when he became aware of Sarah standing at the door.

'Sarah! You naughty girl! You should be in bed.'

Her lips puckered. 'Not tired,' she said.

'Now that's two whole words you have strung together! It must be my influence. Did you come down to show off?'

Sarah had no wish to pursue the subject. She lurched across the room and stood by his chair. 'Baby,' she pointed.

'That's right. I'm reading about babies, and I've a book here by a doctor called Benjamin Spock which is all about looking after babies. From its pristine condition, I deduce that your mother didn't fancy it, which strikes me as a shame. If she had done, you might have learned to stay in bed.'

Sarah smiled, stroking his hand. 'Drink,' she suggested.

'All right. I could do with a shot myself.'

When they were settled again on the rug, he said, 'Now, as soon as I've finished this, you're going upstairs. Got that? I'm not in the mood for chat. You see, Sarah, though I've been reading all evening — and it's good, sensational stuff — the bloody brain has been ticking over with something different and I can't get rid of it.'

Sarah looked miserable. 'Mung. Story,' she pleaded.

'I'll tell you a story. Only it's not the sort you are after. It starts halfway through, I suppose, this afternoon up on the moor. A girl said something to me, and I can't get it out of my mind. She said that if she explained, I would say she was trying to involve me, and she wasn't. It was entirely her fault. In other words, she's a bit like your mother, independent. But that's not the reason I mention it.'

He fiddled with his glass, not looking at his audience. 'There was a party and she was upset after what R.G. had said, and I realized too late, and then I was all over Julia, and then this one went for Ellard — a sort of reaction — and that wasn't all. Of course, it is possible that nothing happened, but if it did, it could have been as a result of the way I behaved. That's it, my girl. You will appreciate why I've got plenty to think about. Now it's time for you to go back to bed.'

'Not a story,' she snivelled.

'All I can manage tonight.' Then he saw the time on his watch. 'Hang on. I shan't be a minute.'

The mirror was smeared with thumb marks. He rubbed it impatiently and examined the reflection at the test-tube's base. According to the leaflet, if there was 'a dark, well-formed ring' you were pregnant; if none of the appropriate hormones was present, you could expect only 'a yellowish-red deposit'. While not exactly anticipating the former, he would have preferred the latter to be more decisive. The disc showing in the mirror was murky, shading into brown. Clearly you could not depend on it, and the manufacturers might have been conceding that point in marketing a double kit. But that was not good enough.

'Dear Ladylove Laboratories,' Tom worked out. 'I should like to draw your attention to a fault in your product. After one test, scrupulously conducted, I have discovered that the information on the leaflet is inadequate. There is no illustration of the colour to be expected when the experiment has been carried out upon the urine of a normal, healthy male. Anticipating your objection that the test was not devised for this substance, I must point out that many men today are as interested as women in the latest developments in science and I do not think they should be debarred from access to their more homely applications. I think that this is a matter which contravenes the Sex Discrimination Act and, unless I receive a satisfactory explanation from you, I shall pass on to the Equal Opportunities Commission a full report of my research.'

He pocketed everything he had used and put the remaining test-tube in the box. It was obviously useless. Kate would have to go to a pharmacist. But it was just possible that her symptoms had a psychological cause. Perhaps that was why his test had come out a dirty brown.

Downstairs, Sarah had not moved from the hearthrug. 'Come on,' he said to her, more gently. 'Time for bed.'

She rose, tired and desolate.

'I'm sorry, love. I've told you I've got things on my mind. You can't have my attention all the time. That's what the Spock feller says — parents are human. You have to give them a break now and again.'

She put her arms round his legs and buried her face in his trousers. 'Not naughty,' she mumbled.

'Do you mean me, or you?'

She did not answer but clung more tightly, warming his legs. 'O.K., relax. Before we go up, I'll tell you a story. About a beautiful young lady.' He felt her flinch. 'No, don't take on. You'll like it, this time.'

On the sofa, with Sarah pressing against him, he began. 'Once upon a time there was a little girl called Sarah.'

She looked up at him, smiling. 'Yes. And Tom.'

'If you insist, we'll put him in, too.'

She was asleep before the end of the first paragraph.

Tom reflected that he had not lost his touch. He had a peculiarly soporific effect on the women in this house.

Chapter Thirteen

It was a long time before anyone answered the telephone.

'Yes?' a man yawned.

'May I speak to Kate?'

'Kate? Now?' There was a pause, then a reluctant, 'Very well. I'll fetch her.'

Another long wait.

Kate's voice. 'Yes?'

'Hello. This is Tom.'

'Tom?'

This family was a real bunch of zombies. 'Kate, I've been thinking.'

'You've called me up to tell me that?'

'Can I see you?'

'What, *now*?'

'Christ! You do make things difficult.'

'Tom, do you realize that we were all asleep?'

'Bully for you. I didn't have the pleasure, last night. I want to talk to you.'

'What about?'

'What you told me yesterday.'

'I don't wish to discuss it.'

'I don't think that is very constructive. You can't sit around and do nothing.'

'Exactly.' Her voice rose. 'That is why I'm thinking of having an abortion.'

'An abortion? Where's your telephone?'

'What's that to do with it?'

'You were shouting. Or have you already told your parents?'

'No, but I think they suspect. They'll probably think it's you. Fellers don't generally call before dawn.' She giggled, too long.

'But, Kate, it's sickening. I've been reading it up.'

'So have I, man. But it may have to happen.'

'Not necessarily. Kids aren't so bad.'

'Except that you have to look after them. It's all right for men. None of the graft.'

'A lot of men help bring up their children.'

'Only they don't give up their jobs. Or university.'

'There are crèches for kids in most colleges now.'

'Are you seriously suggesting that I drag down with a baby to Cambridge? Because that's where I'm set on going.'

'I'm trying to work out the alternatives.'

'I already have. Look, Tom, I wish you didn't interfere.'

He winced. 'That's not how I would express it.'

'Oh, all right. So you are trying to help.'

'Why do you have to be so bloody graceless?'

'Graceless? Now that's a laugh.' She gave a demonstration. It went on some time. 'I'm sorry I can't manage more grace, I'm having a hard enough job to appear normal.'

Tom forbore to comment that she had an odd definition of normality. 'I know. It must be rotten.'

'Oh, piss off. Why of all people does it have to be you bothering me? I was getting on all right till I saw you yesterday.'

'You can hardly blame me for that. I wasn't chasing you.'

172

'You can say that again,' she answered, sharp and accusing. Then, quieter, 'I'm not blaming you, Tom. You're in the clear. It's always been just me.'

He was conscious of his breathing. The base of his spine had begun to tingle. The handset was slippery in his grasp. Perhaps it was that 'always'. 'I'm not sure what you are telling me,' he said.

'Telling you?' Her tone had changed again. It was defensive, harsh. 'I'm only saying that it is my business. I'll get through it. I think we'd better ring off.'

'Meet me by Nether Gill. In half an hour.'

'I'm already committed. We are going to Sheffield to see my grandmother.'

Grandmothers in Sheffield ought to be banned. 'Tonight, then?'

'I've said I don't want to meet you.'

'I'll expect you at seven.'

'All right, if that will shut you up. But seven is too early.'

'Half past?'

'No, eight.'

Did they always bargain like this? 'O.K. Be there.'

'I will.'

At least he could be sure that she would keep her word.

You had to be firm with some women, though he did not know why he was making the effort. After a lifetime resisting Belinda, he must be a devil for punishment to tangle with another shrew, when you thought about it. Tom did so, as he stripped off his sweatshirt and trousers. (They looked tired after the night's wear.) His was probably a classic case of conditioning (peeling off his socks and inhaling their fragrance). Years of fighting Belinda had developed his reflexes (admiring the exotic

173

pattern of his briefs). If a woman put up a fight, he would automatically take her on. Jonquil fought differently, by evasion, but he would consider that later. When he had had some sleep.

But with Belinda around you could not rely on that.

'Tom!' she shouted, standing by his bed. 'I've been calling ages! Someone for you on the telephone.'

As he slid down to the hall, still dreaming, he imagined she had already returned from Sheffield.

'You having a lay-in?' R.G. asked.

'What time is it?' Surely he had not missed her.

'About one o'clock. Just wanting to know whether you would like a lift up this evening. Lovely party she is putting together.'

Lovely party... This evening. He had forgotten! 'Thanks, but you had better not bother. As things are going, I may be late.'

'You've got over seven hours before then!'

'Yes, but there is something I've got on at eight, so I'll go to Jonquil's from there.'

'Well, if you take my advice, you won't be too late. Cliff Turnbull was there this morning, making himself useful, and by the way he was behaving I'd say he is a man with nasty designs.'

'He always is. But thanks for the hint.'

Seven hours before she would be up at Nether Gill! They stretched like a life sentence without remission and he could not imagine how he would fill them in.

Lunch, extended by inconsequent chat of two carefree parents, might have taken care of an hour or so, but as it happened he soon put an end to it. The chat on offer was the sort he could do without.

'I had a very odd experience this morning,' Mike began, as he recycled his mince. 'I was roused by a

174

strange noise and staggered on to the landing, debating whether it was the dawn chorus, in which case I was in for a unique experience, or whether it was some radio-controlled burglar, in which case I'd go back to bed. I soon discovered that neither deduction was correct.'

'I had to make a telephone call,' Tom interrupted, hoping to stem the flow.

'So I concluded, and I searched for an explanation. Was it possible that after all these years I had misunderstood my son? Instead of sleeping round the clock and not rising until noon, did he spend those hours when the world was dew-fresh offering advice to young ladies? Shocked, I retreated, but not – I have to confess to you – before a few stray words reached me. I'm sorry about that, Tom.'

'That's all right, Mike,' he said, putting down his fork. He wondered what it was about Belinda's cooking which could so stimulate Mike's prose.

'I don't like to comment on something overheard.'

'In that case, spare yourself.'

'I don't think I can do that. I am bound to be involved some time. After our conversation on Thursday I was worried, but I never imagined this.'

'We shall have to speak to her parents,' Belinda supported him.

'Are you suggesting that I have something to do with it?'

'Well, haven't you? Look, Tom, don't try to prevaricate. Just come clean.'

'Come clean! You and Belinda are behaving as if I ought to get married!'

'I neither mentioned nor implied that.'

'Good. Because I'm not interested. I never have been, despite Belinda's pressure.'

175

'Whatever are you talking about?' she demanded.

'I'm very confused,' Mike said. 'Aren't you jumping a few stages? No one has said anything about marriage yet.'

'And neither has she, if you want to know,' Tom shouted, pushing back his plate. 'So be satisfied with that, if you can.' And, not caring whether or not they misinterpreted him, he left the table and rushed from the house.

A T-shirt is an inadequate garment for mid October in a town scythed by draughts from the moor, but for a time insulation was provided by anger. When that wore off he rubbed at the goosepimples and wondered how he could pass the afternoon. There should be ways of serving time, even in this place: one, you could slip into the bookshop and skim through a volume; two, you could sit in the library and catch up with the news; or three, in the annual exhibition of local artists, you could check that Yorkshire was still green, sinking under drystone walls and riddled with sheep. Tom turned into Woolworth's to examine the display of pop records.

But before he reached them, he bumped into Dave.

It was impossible to avoid him, though he did attempt to, by stepping over a pushchair and thrusting aside two dogs, but this provoked objections so he lost valuable time.

'I saw that,' Dave told him. 'You may not want to meet me but you don't have to make it so obvious.'

'I'll do better next time.'

'I suppose you couldn't spare a second to put me in the picture? Though I ought to be demanding an apology. I don't like being called a dirty little shit.'

'You'll have to get used to it if you slap people you know into books.'

'It's unavoidable, for this one, but you needn't worry. I shan't try to publish. It's too personal.'

'You surprise me. I'd have thought it would be nothing but objective dissection.'

'Objective! I wish it could be. I expected you might take this line. If it had been anyone else, I'd have told you earlier, though you'd still have laughed.'

'I can't see what there is to laugh at.'

'There isn't, but you might have had a go. Yesterday, after that telephone call, I tried to see it from your point of view. I said to myself, if Tom fancied my mother, how should I react? But the trouble was, I couldn't get the feel of it. I simply couldn't imagine your being turned on by her. So the exercise wasn't any help.'

It was no help to Tom, either, but to keep possibilities open, he volunteered, 'Your mother isn't bad, Dave.'

'She's all right, as a mother. But who would go for her as a mistress? Whereas, Belinda . . .'

'Belinda?' He thought he would never catch up, so he repeated the name several times, trying to get it to fit. At last he managed, 'I thought you meant Jonquil.'

'Jonquil? Who's she?'

Tom looked round. There are moments when Woolworth's is an unsuitable environment for intimate discussion. 'Can we start this again from scratch? Do you think we could manage to solicit a beer?'

'I don't fancy soliciting anything else at the moment. Let's try The Crags. Steve Linthwaite has left and, after all, I am eighteen next month. We'll negotiate a post-dated pint.'

Steve Linthwaite's replacement was new to the town so he was not yet linked up to the bush telegraph. Provided that you had the cash, he would pull you a pint. In fact, he had no objection to pulling several during the next twenty minutes, and when he called for last orders Tom added another to their stock. 'Thirsty work, discussing erotica,' he confided happily.

'She ever come in here?' the new barman asked.

Finally, out on the pavement, Dave said, 'Pleased we've got that straight.'

'It's the only thing that is,' Tom answered, peering into the crowd which rotated at the perimeter of his vision.

'It's the beer. Contaminated. They pour the drip-trays back into the barrels. Think . . . I'll be going to bed. To sleep it off. You coming?'

'No, thanks. I'll make shift with my own.'

They moved carefully up the main street, but there was a good deal of opposition to their progress. 'We'll be all right when we get to the top,' Dave encouraged.

There, he said to Tom, 'Right. Now I'll shog off. Pleased I've told you . . . about Belinda. Clears the air . . . Never imagined you in the same plight . . . The Julia confused. Sorry you're having second thoughts.'

'Never had first thoughts, as I said.'

'No, not about her. The other – what's her name? Do you think you ever properly fancied her? Not just turned on by the situation?'

'There wasn't one. So it must have been her. I fancied her . . . I still do . . . I must fancy her . . . See what I mean? Got to.'

'She's throwing a party tonight.'

'I'm going.'

'Best of luck, then.' Dave stepped away, then turned back. 'Tom, when I've finished this book, would you read it? There may be things . . . comment on.'

'Delighted.' They stood together while the world spun round them and Tom resisted the impulse to put an arm round Dave's shoulder. (The town's vigilantes were out in force.)

It was this mood which caused Tom to behave as he did five minutes later. Passing the street leading to the police station, he saw three men entering its doors. They were engaged in an unequal skirmish. Despite his rolling vision, Tom easily picked that up. Two constables were pushing a man who gesticulated wildly. There were flashes of orange plastic, Goodenough's last signals to Life Outside.

It was surprising how quickly his brain could function, Tom told himself as he stepped across the road. He had deduced immediately the meaning of that little scene. They were taking Roland Goodenough in for questioning. They had made sure of grabbing him when he was wearing the donkey jacket. He had been calling on Tom to help him. He could not have chosen a better man. Stimulated by a forty-minute discussion with Dave and strengthened by three (or was it four?) pints of the best draught, he would soon put the fuzz straight. 'Hang on, Goodenough,' he called. 'Here I come,' as he fell down the step into the office.

But Goodenough had not been allowed to wait for him; they had taken him straight to a cell. However, one of the constables lingered, resting tired elbows on the desk as he greeted the visitor.

'Easy to miss that step. What can I do for you?'

'I should like to see Mr Goodenough.'

'He won't be long. He's in with the sergeant.'

'That's why I'm here.'

'That so?'

'Defence Counsel.'

The constable looked at him warily. 'Aren't you Mike Taylor's lad?'

'He's my father. Look, do you mind if I sit down?'

'Do that. I reckon you've been on the booze.'

'What gives you that idea?'

'I ask the questions, mate.' He got up, opened a door and spoke through it without removing his eyes from Tom. 'Cyril, can you spare a minute?'

'Well, if it isn't Belinda Taylor's lad,' Cyril Todd greeted.

'She's my mother.' It was wearisome, all this need for correction.

'How is she?'

'Fine.' Adding, to complete the file, 'So am I.'

'I can see that. Been having a few jars?'

These policemen either worked by telepathy or had one-track minds, Tom concluded, sighing.

Cyril Todd joined him. 'It's a bad thing, drink, at your age.'

'At any age, surely.'

'Not when it's legal. Good thing I didn't catch you at it. We'll have to make do with a caution,' he compromised sadly.

'That's not what I'm here for.' If they put Counsel through it like this, Tom keened gently to himself, what happened when they came to his client?

'You leave it to Sergeant Todd to decide what you're here for,' the constable advised.

'I'd nip you back home but the panda's in dock,' Cyril Todd said. 'Tell you what, there's Mr Goodenough inside. Perhaps he could help.'

'How much is his bail?' Tom asked.

They ignored him.

Goodenough, fetched from the interior, showed his concern, then moved on to the defence. He appeared to be suffering from role dissonance. 'I think you should know that there are mitigating circumstances in this case, Sergeant. The young man has been under considerable strain recently. Professional etiquette prevents my saying more than that the matter is known to my colleagues and is receiving attention. This is just the sort of occurrence that some of us feared.'

'It happens,' Cyril Todd said, looking at his watch.

'Before I accompany Taylor home, Sergeant, may I refer briefly to our interrupted dialogue? I most sincerely appreciate your open receptivity to my request. An informal symposium on alcohol and its attendant risks, innovated by yourself or one of your staff, would, you will agree from the sorry example we have before us, be a most invaluable module in my unit: "Drink — Adults with a Purpose".'

This speech was shorter than Tom had expected, allowing little time for a kip on the floor.

'Get up, Tom. Try to walk, there's a good fellow,' Goodenough pleaded. 'Hasn't he a jacket? He probably pawned it, for the drink,' creating a pawn shop to fill a need. 'You can't go home like that, Tom. Here, I'll lend you this.'

Tom regarded the donkey jacket held in front of him. There was a connection somewhere. Slowly, wishing he had brought a pillow, he said, 'You can't get rid of it that way, like a hot wallet. They're not that daft. I know I was the one to persuade you to take it, but I'm not having all the responsibility. There are limits, whatever Belinda says.'

'He's raving,' the constable diagnosed.

'No, feverish,' Goodenough corrected inaccurately. 'Help me to get it on.'

It was no use struggling against them. Nor was it

possible to shake off Goodenough's commiserating hand on the somnambulant plod home.

'I'll telephone your parents later,' the man promised when he had finally accepted that they were out. 'Not in a spirit of complaint or condemnation, please understand that, Tom, but in order that they do not misinterpret what has occurred.'

In his room, Tom hooked the donkey jacket on his door before falling on to the bed. The orange patches hung above him, as they had done at R.G.'s party. A guilt coming home to roost.

It took him a few seconds to work out the silence and darkness. He must have slept through. He had missed her. Three thirty, by the luminous hands of his watch, until, his ear to it, he realized that it had stopped. Racing downstairs, he peered at the clock in the kitchen. Half past seven. Night or morning? A note from his mother: 'We have gone out and may end up at Leeds Playhouse, then go for a meal. Pity you were not back before we left. You might have liked to come.' Fancy that! Belinda inviting him out! Theatre, then free nosh. Was this the first hint of a maternal inclination? She was probably cracking up. And so would he be, soon. The telephone rang: Goodenough, asking to speak to his father. 'Sorry, wrong number,' he answered and took the stairs in three leaps.

He could get there in ten minutes, if he went at a good lick. One trouble about being a lover, he said to himself as he turned on the shower, is that you get into bad habits. One: you pay too much attention to washing, whereas there's many a woman who would fancy you whether or not you were clean. Lots are not so particular themselves. Take Liz, for instance. Except that she had managed a bit of a spit and polish for Stan. Second habit he ought to get under control was changing his clothes so often. A woman might assume that a high standard of laundering was expected of her later, which might discourage her if she were anything like Belinda. Third habit was rehearsing what you were going to say to her (what do you say to a girl who is pregnant?) and working out the moves, particularly the end-game when you want to be sure of mate. Fourth habit was heavy breathing. That last he was absolutely unable to cure.

It continued as he went through the town and was not caused by the pace he was going at; by now he knew the difference between this affliction and simple lack of breath. But she will think it is that I've been running, he said to himself as, leaving the street lamps, he turned on to the track. Stars lit the last sprint and helped him find a path through the fern as he looped round the gill. Then at the top, under the trees, it was black.

'Heavens, Tom! You must be out of condition,' a voice said.

'Depends what condition you are referring to,' he managed, adding silently, I've been in this one for weeks.

'You needn't have hurried. In fact, I tried to prevent you. I telephoned when I got back from Sheffield, but there was no answer.'

'I'm pleased about that because I wouldn't have let you off. I must have been asleep.'

'Wouldn't you? But why asleep?'

'I'd had a few pints with Dave.'

'Oh, of course. He phoned me. Just after I got in.'

Only a little light fluttered through the branches, showing her against the bole of a tree. He wanted to see her face.

'Let's sit here,' stepping to the edge of the spinney and selecting a boulder. 'I can't talk to a dark blob.'

She laughed as she joined him.

'Look, Kate, I've got something to say to you.'

He paused, considering. For one thing, he did not know how to say it, and for another he was anxious about her reaction. When you examined it, the last five weeks did not offer much help. He had tried just about everything: scheming, extracting addresses from secretaries, insinuating himself into flats on the pretext of questionnaires, studying plays, wrestling with flower arrangements, skipping lessons, reading up pregnancy, baby-sitting, setting up scientific experiments. But he had not rehearsed this. And all the hard labour should have given him an idea of how a woman would respond, but it did not. This was disappointing. It made you question the whole concept of vocational training.

'It sounds ominous,' Kate prompted.

On the other hand, surely he could claim that he had gathered a few clues about women on the way? He had tangled with more – a whole coven – than he would have thought possible inside five weeks. You could not count Belinda; she was a constant, but even so, the Stan bit had startled him. Then there were Julia and Jonquil. And Liz, whom he would always think of with affection. And Sarah . . .

Abruptly, he told her, 'Kate, I think you should marry me.'

'What?'

'You heard.' Embarrassed, he explained, 'I'm offering to make an honest woman of you.'

'I've never been dishonest,' she answered sharply. Then she began to laugh, but the laughter was not hysterical. It was deep-throated and free. 'I'm sorry,

Tom. I'm not laughing at you. It must be the fashion. You're the third one this week.'

Which proves how little you can anticipate answers. 'The third?' How many men had she had?

'R.G. was the first.'

'R.G.?'

'Obviously, I couldn't accept him, even if I had wanted to get married, knowing how he is gone on me. Then there was Dave this afternoon.'

'Dave?'

'For heaven's sake, stop echoing me like a parrot. Yes, Dave. But he was drunk. Are you?'

'Never been more sober.'

'I hope you have. It is not the proposition of a sober man.'

'Perhaps I am drunk, but not with beer. What about it?'

'About it? Getting married? Tom, you must be going bananas. You don't go into something like that on a whim. In any case, it is no longer pertinent. That's why I tried to get through to you. There was no need for you to meet me. I'm not pregnant. I started this afternoon.'

'Thank goodness.'

'You can say that again. It's been hanging over me for what seems like weeks. I feel like a lifer suddenly reprieved.'

'Are you sure?'

'As sure as I can be at present. The whole business must have given a jolt to my insides and thrown me out.'

For a reason he could not stop to work out, their frank talk did not surprise him.

'There are those pregnancy kits. They have two goes, but even then I'm not sure they are reliable.'

'What makes you say that?'

'I've tried one. Look.' He fished into his jacket pocket and drew out the test-tube he had placed there the previous night. The contents looked unhealthy; some particles had risen and formed a thin crust. 'Looks as if it's growing a culture,' he observed anxiously.

This time he joined her in laughter. It rolled them about on the boulder together, bringing them close.

'You're a clown,' she said finally.

'I don't see why. It's an obvious line of investigation.'

'Well, yes. But probably the kit was faulty,' she consoled, still laughing. 'Honestly, you kill me.'

'It's an effect I have. Liz says that, too.'

'Liz?'

'The woman I baby-sit for.'

'Oh, yes. I've heard. It must be pleasant to have so many people appreciative.' She got up and stood looking at the lit town below them. 'I'd better go now. I don't want to make you late for your next engagement.'

'Who told you about that?'

'Dave. He told me quite a bit, but he was drunk and confusing, so I didn't follow everything. Anyway, I'm sorry you came all this way for nothing, Tom.'

He nodded. It was irrational, but he could not suppress his disappointment.

Turning away, she said, 'You make me feel like something out of a Victorian novel, a fallen woman. I really cherish that, offering to make an honest woman of me! Even R.G. didn't put it like that.'

Again he felt an irrational tremor: jealousy. 'Perhaps he has had more experience in such matters.'

'What a bloody thing to say!' She swung round to him. 'He really meant what he said.'

'And you suggest that I didn't? That's an equally bloody thing to imply.' He rose, angry. 'You can't even say thank you!'

'Is that what you want, to be thanked?' she shouted up at him. 'Is that the reason you offered? Do you know, just for a moment, I thought it might be for more than that. Sorry,' she said, quieter. 'That wasn't fair. I'm going.'

'Not yet,' blocking her way. 'We'll have a fight, if you want one, Kate. I reckon we're pretty compatible in that. But not for a minute, if you can just hang on. There are one or two questions I want to ask.'

'You've no right.'

'I'm not concerned with legalities.'

'No one has.'

'Not even the father?'

'There isn't one. Remember?'

'But you thought there was, when R.G. asked you. Was it his?'

'For heaven's sake! There isn't a baby!'

'Don't be evasive. Why didn't you accept?'

'I've told you. I don't love him. I'm orthodox enough to want that.'

'So you don't entirely rule out marriage. And it was.'

'No, it wasn't. God, you've got me talking like you! If there had been one, it wouldn't have been his.'

'Or Dave's?'

'Give me strength! He was drunk.'

'So the father never offered.'

'He didn't know. It was none of his business.'

'Isn't that taking Women's Lib a bit far?'

'I'll take it as far as I like. Which means I won't be beholden to any man.'

'Christ, Kate! You're like Liz.'

'No, I'm not. I don't have young men in my room till all hours.'

'Where did you get that from?'

'After two o'clock, wasn't it, last Friday?'

'I don't know. I didn't bother to check. You're a shrew, Kate.'

'And you won't tame me.'

'I don't want to.'

Exhausted, they stood in silence, and he dropped his hands from her arms. If this was a foretaste of what was in store for him, Tom reflected, he would have to stay off the beer and get more rest.

'She went to sleep. But in any case, I'd decided against it,' he told her.

'You don't have to give explanations. I'm not offering them to you.'

'No, but I want you to know.'

'I'll tell you about this one day, when it is further behind me.'

'I think I can guess.'

'And now there's another party.'

'Dave managed to give you a lot of background detail, didn't he, despite his condition? I hope that he mentioned that most of it is out of date.' He bent over her, breathing in the smell of her hair. 'I wasn't raving, you know. I wasn't going into it on a whim.'

'I'm afraid that is how I went into it.'

'Kate, would you have said yes to me if there had been a baby?'

He wished he could see her. They were untouched by the starlight, under the trees.

'I don't suppose so. No.'

'For the same reason that you refused R.G.?'

She was still, leaning against him. 'You ask too many questions.'

'I don't. Kate, I have to know. Would you have refused me for the same reason you did R.G.?'

There was a pause. 'You must be dim, Thomas Taylor, if you really don't know the answer to that.'

It was strange how easily his arms went round her. There are some things, given the right moment, you do not need to rehearse.

'Are you growing a beard?' she asked later.

'Yes.' Then, apprehensive, remembering, 'Why? Is it ticklish?'

Her answer seemed a long time coming. 'No, abrasive. But I prefer it that way.'

Would you like to hear about my book club?

It's for 4-8 year-olds and you get your own badge, membership book and a Club magazine four times a year.

It's packed with stories, puzzles and competitions.

The Egg

You get a chance to buy new books!

And there's lots more! For further details and an application form send a stamped, addressed envelope to:

The Junior Puffin Club,
P. O. Box 21,
Cranleigh,
Surrey,
GU6 8UZ